KENNETT HIGH SCHOOL

Date _____ # _____

THE YEAR THEY BURNED THE BOOKS

NANCY GARDEN

The Year They Burned the Books

FARRAR STRAUS GIROUX

NEW YORK

The events in this story are not based on events in any one specific town.

Copyright © 1999 by Nancy Garden
All rights reserved
Distributed in Canada by Douglas & McIntyre Ltd.
Printed in the United States of America
Designed by Filomena Tuosto
First edition, 1999
12 11 10 9 8

Library of Congress Cataloging-in-Publication Data
Garden, Nancy.
    The year they burned the books / Nancy Garden. — 1st ed.
        p.   cm.
    Summary: While trying to come to terms with her own lesbian
feelings, Jamie, a high-school senior and editor of the school
newspaper, finds herself in the middle of a battle with a group of
townspeople over the new health education curriculum.
    ISBN 0-374-38667-6
    [1. Journalism—Fiction.   2. Homosexuality—Fiction.
3. Censorship—Fiction.   4. Prejudices—Fiction.   5. High schools—
Fiction.   6. Schools—Fiction.]   I. Title.
PZ7.G165Ye   1999
[Fic]—dc21   98–43483

To the courageous plaintiffs,

librarians,

and lawyers

who saved ANNIE ON MY MIND

from being permanently banned

in the Olathe, Kansas, School District,

with thanks and love!

September

ONE

Despite a foggy beginning, it had become too nice a day—a soft September afternoon—to be cooped up arguing in the Wilson High *Telegraph*'s tiny office. Being the paper's editor in chief was a goal for which Jamie Crawford had been striving ever since she'd started high school. That part felt good, but being in the middle of an argument between her two best friends didn't feel good at all.

"It's a matter of life or death, you jerk!" sports editor Terry Gage was shouting as he pounded his desk with a strong, impatient hand.

"No, it's not, Terry," Nomi Pembar insisted, glaring at him. "It's a matter of right and wrong." Nomi was art editor and dressed so carefully she often pressed her jeans as well as the flowered blouses she usually wore.

"Look," Jamie told them, "it doesn't really matter what we think about it." She leaned forward in her chair, her small, even features solemn, her dark eyes intense under her brown bangs. "What matters is that the whole school's talking about it, and the paper has to have an opinion."

"Spoken like a true editor." Matthew Caggin, who taught sophomore and junior English and was also the paper's faculty adviser, came into the office, balancing a full mug of coffee on top of a pile of uncorrected English papers. Behind him was Cindy Nash, the paper's ad manager and occasional reporter, a short, cheerful junior with an infectious laugh. The gray baseball cap that her boyfriend, Jack Kellog, also a junior and the paper's star reporter, had given her the year before was perched jauntily back-to-front on her short blond curls. Jack, who'd been voted best-dressed sophomore boy the year before, frequently worked in the office with the editors. But today he was off interviewing a student who'd been caught in a bad August storm on his father's lobster boat.

Nomi balanced on the stool in front of the battered layout table. "But handing out condoms is a moral issue, Matt, and . . ."

"And you don't all agree about it. That's good, gang; don't you get that yet?" Matt put his papers down and took a sip of coffee before he folded himself carefully onto his chair. Matt stood over six feet in his socks and walked with a slight stoop, as if constantly looking out for low doorways.

"I get it," Cindy said. "Newspapers should represent all sides of things." She handed Nomi an envelope. "Here's some early ads. I started collecting right after that planning meeting we had before school started."

"I get it, too," Terry said, smiling. "And Jamie gets it, but Nomi—well, we all know how artists are."

"That's not fair!" Nomi tossed her head angrily, making her red hair cascade over her shoulders. She dumped the ads out onto the layout table. "And that's not the issue, anyway. I thought editorials were supposed to represent the paper's opinion, not just Jamie's."

"Not necessarily, Nomi," Matt corrected gently. "It's nice if we can all agree, but there's nothing in our policy that says editorials can't be just the editor in chief's opinion."

"Hey." Jamie put her hand on Nomi's arm. "Cool it, Nom'. Terry was kidding. And anyway, I agree we should represent both sides editorially. Why don't you write us an op-ed if you feel so strongly?"

"Bring in religion, morality," Cindy suggested without sarcasm. "You could do that real well, Nomi."

"Saving yourself for your one true love," Terry put in, and hummed the wedding march.

Nomi glared at him again, and this time so did Jamie.

"Good idea, Cindy." Matt put down his coffee mug. "Perfect, in fact. Now look, we've got to . . ."

A shadow appeared against the puckered glass window in the office door, and when the door opened, Jamie saw a tall, dark-skinned girl framed in the entrance. Tiny silver stars, linked together like paper chains, dangled, glittering, from her ears; a matching star, even tinier, glittered from her left nostril. A bright red cape, fastened at the throat with a huge hook and eye wrapped in black silk thread, was draped casually over her otherwise standard clothes—jeans, long-sleeved scoop-neck T-shirt.

"You the editor?" the girl asked, looking right at Jamie.

"Editor in chief," Terry said, and Jamie nodded, speechless.

The girl seemed amused. "Are you staring because I'm beautiful or because I'm strange?"

"B-both," Jamie managed to say with an embarrassed laugh. Nomi rolled her eyes, Cindy chuckled, and Jamie heard Terry murmur "Mmm" softly. "I mean, I well . . ."

The girl made a broad gesture with a graceful hand. Silver rings circled several of her fingers, and her nails were covered with dark polish, maybe black, maybe purple. "That's the best answer yet," she said. "Most honest, anyway."

Cindy gave her a friendly smile. "Welcome."

The girl studied Cindy for a second, as if deciding how to react, then said, "Thank you."

Nomi stood, all business. "I bet you're here about the photo editor's job. I'm Nomi Pembar, the art editor, which means I do layout, position ads, and occasionally draw something. That's Terry Gage"—Terry gave a little bow—"the sports editor. Cindy Nash is ad manager, although once in a while she writes. And that's Matt Caggin, faculty adviser. He's an English teacher, but we get to call him Matt in the newspaper office. Got any pictures to show us?"

The girl slid the strap of a blue-green portfolio off her shoulder. "Yes. I'm Tessa Gillespie, by the way. Tess, usually."

"The new senior," said Matt, stating it, not asking. "From Boston. Welcome!" He stuck out his hand, and Tessa shook it formally.

Jamie tried not to go on staring. She'd heard rumors that a Boston family with a high-school-age daughter was moving to their small New England coastal town. But she hadn't seen anyone new yesterday, which had been the first day of classes, so she'd assumed they hadn't come. And then the condom fight had taken over her attention.

Tessa smiled wryly and slid a stack of 8×10 glossies out of her portfolio. "Thank you again." She spread the photos on Nomi's table: kids playing in water that sprayed from a fire hydrant, a cat on a window ledge, EMTs rushing a stretcher away from a building—city photos, sharp and active.

"Great!" Jamie exclaimed, and Terry and Cindy nodded.

Matt was studying the EMT photo. "Tell you what, Tessa. Spend a couple of days shooting around town. Give us three pictures. Let us see what interests you, what kind of news nose you have. Okay?"

"Sure." Tessa returned the photos to her portfolio, then swept the air in front of her as if indicating a headline. Her rings, one of which Jamie saw was a band of stars, caught the sunlight coming through the dusty window over Matt's desk. "Town of Wilson, through the eyes of a stranger."

Matt nodded. "Good. Nice meeting you, Tessa. You get the photos to us by the end of the week. We'll review them along with the others that come in and let you know. Good luck."

Tessa's answering nod was brief and crisp. "Okay. See you." She moved to the door. "Soon."

Terry whistled when she'd gone. "Whoa! That is one weird sure-of-herself woman!" He winked at Jamie.

"I like her," Cindy said decisively. "She'll have to be sure of herself to survive here looking like that." She giggled. "Wait till Jack sees her. I bet his mouth'll drop open."

Nomi frowned. "She seems a little too sure of herself and a little too weird. Like, what's she hiding, you know?"

"That's not the point," Jamie snapped; she was intrigued with Tessa's outward oddness, and she'd immediately felt drawn to her, although Terry's wink made her self-conscious about that. "The point is, would she make a good photo editor?"

"The other point," Matt said gently, "is, could you guys work with her?"

"Yes," said Jamie. "How about you, Nomi? You're the art editor."

"I'm not sure yet."

"Oh, come on, Nomi," Cindy said. "I bet she'll lighten up when she gets to know us. After all"—she grinned—"we're pretty special people. The elite of Wilson High." She doffed her baseball cap and made a deep bow.

Terry swung his chair around. "So maybe she's got an attitude. So what? Her photos are good. I say let's give her a try."

"No need to decide yet," Matt reminded them. "Let's see what she comes up with. There *are* other applicants, after all. Now, about this condom thing. What do we have so far that's related to it?"

Jamie riffled through the papers on her desk, glad to be able to concentrate on something else. "A few standard school-opening pieces from the other reporters, but Jack did a great story about the new health education curriculum, with a list of what's going to be taught in each grade . . ."

"Including middle school and elementary?" Matt asked her. "Or just us?"

"Just us, but I could get you middle school easily, since my mom teaches social studies there; she was on the committee that worked on the health ed stuff. And I could send a reporter to the elementary school."

"What do you think?"

"I think that's the job of the town paper, not us. We cover the high school, not all of Wilson."

"Yeah," Terry agreed. "We start doing that, next thing you know I'll have to cover middle-school sports, and then pretty soon I'll be writing about hide-and-seek in first grade. No thanks!"

"Okay," said Matt, ignoring Cindy's appreciative giggle. "Agreed. So that's it, Jamie? Just Jack's curriculum story?"

"Right, and the storm-at-sea interview he's doing now, if

he finishes it on time, plus a press release announcing the distribution—I guess it's not really distribution, exactly—saying condoms will be available in the nurse's office every Friday after dismissal."

Terry chuckled. "In time for the weekend."

"That's disgusting!" Nomi exploded. "It's almost asking kids to go out and have sex on the weekend!"

"Say that in your op-ed piece, Nom'," Jamie said mildly. "Say it in your piece."

"Maybe I'll do just that," Nomi said angrily, turning back to the layout table.

"Atta girl, Nom'," Jamie said. "Go for it."

The warm September air had cooled to crispness by 4:30, when Jamie and Terry left the newspaper office; Nomi and Cindy had already gone home. There'd been no return of the thickish fog that had rolled in early that morning from the ocean and snaked its way across the cluster of white clapboard shops and houses in Wilson's small center and down the side streets radiating from it. Jamie's family, and Terry's, too, lived near the working harbor, where the fishermen kept their boats, down the coast a bit from the fancy yacht basin, which was still dotted with pleasure craft, though it was after Labor Day. Tourists came to Wilson well into October; they were just a different kind of tourist from the summer variety— older, with bigger boats or, if they were landlubbers, huge RVs with license-plate bouquets astern. The RVs made the town seem more crowded than it really was as they lumbered along its narrow main street and held up traffic entering the interstate a few miles away. Jamie was always glad when they left and Wilson pulled back into itself, settling down for the winter like a close nuclear family after the holiday guests have gone home. And she was glad Terry was around again; he'd been working on his father's lobster boat all summer and had told her he was so tired during the little time he had off that all he wanted to do was veg out at his parents' lakeside cabin. She was looking forward to seeing him every day now that school had started.

"So," Terry asked as they walked away from the town center, "what do you think?"

"About the condom editorial? I've pretty much got it worked out in my mind, but . . ."

"No, dummy. About Tessa." He poked her in the ribs. "Man, did you ever stutter!"

Jamie felt herself blush. "Yeah, I know. Was it really that obvious?"

"To me, your fellow Maybe, yes. To her, I doubt it. By the way," he added, "this is as good a time as any to tell you I think I'm moving from Maybe to Probably."

Jamie looked up at him, startled. It had been back in sixth grade that she and Terry had discovered each other. One day, walking home from school, Jamie had come upon him huddled near a stone wall, bruised and crying—the victim, it turned out, of class bully Brandon Tomkins and his best friend, Al Checkers, who had attacked Jamie the week before. Jamie's dad had taught her a few punches, and Jamie taught them to Terry after taking him to her house so her mother could clean him up. "I can't go home," Terry had sobbed. "My dad'll be there, and he'll be mad I didn't fight back."

"Now you *will* fight back," Jamie had said after they'd sparred a bit. "And I will, too. We'll practice."

The physical bullying had stopped soon after they began

returning the blows they received, and Terry and Jamie became friends. But the verbal taunts continued. What had begun as "lard-ass" for Terry, who'd been overweight till fourth grade, and "nerd-brain" for Jamie, who rarely got below an A–, quickly shifted to "fag" and "Hey, butch." Jamie had always felt different in some undefined way, but eventually, when she tried and failed to be like her suddenly boy-crazy and clothes-conscious classmates, she began to understand why, and the more she understood, the more the name-calling hurt and frightened her. Her mother kept saying Jamie felt different because journalism was so important to her—even then, the walls of her room were covered with news photos and headlines. And her friend Nomi said the kids who teased her were just mean and didn't know any better. But Jamie was increasingly sure there was more to it than that. At least when she got to know Terry, she realized she wasn't the only person who felt cut off from just about everyone else—even sometimes, in a vague, undefined way, from her own family, despite her love for them.

Later, freshman year in high school, after FAGGOT had appeared more than once on the inside of Terry's homeroom desktop, and after Marsha Stevens, captain of the girls' basketball team, had told the other players to watch out for Jamie in the locker room, Jamie and Terry started going out together, "in self-defense," as Terry'd termed it. They'd both gained some status, too, by writing for the paper, Jamie because she'd turned out to have a talent for reporting as well as a passion for newspapers, and Terry because he'd found he was able to make up for his lack of athletic prowess by writing knowledgeably and colorfully about school sports. The verbal assaults diminished a little, but Terry and Jamie, after a long talk one moonlit summer night down on Sloan's Beach, started calling themselves "Maybes"—maybe gay, maybe straight.

"So," said Jamie now, "how come you suddenly think you're a Probably?"

"*Maybe* a Probably," Terry answered.

"How come you're maybe a Probably? Can one be that? I mean, is that allowed? Isn't maybe a Probably still a Maybe?"

"Maybe a Maybe Probably is really a Probably Maybe," Terry retaliated. "No, that doesn't work. Actually," he said, jumping up on the stone wall they were passing, "there are many subtle shades of meaning here. For instance . . ."

"Terry"—Jamie jumped up behind him and held on to his waist for balance as they both teetered along the wall's uneven surface—"why Probably?"

"Because I got to know this wonderful guy last summer who I'd never even noticed before, even though he's been in our class since we were freshmen. I mean, I really *met* him. He was up at the lake a lot . . ." Terry stopped, blushing sheepishly when she tugged at his belt.

"So *that's* why you were never around," Jamie said. " 'I'm so-o-o tired,' " she moaned, mock-imitating him. " 'Lobstering's *such* hard work.' Oh, brother! Hey," she went on when he pulled away. "I'm just kidding. Come on, tell me! I'm glad for you, Terry, really. How'd you get to know him?"

He turned toward her then, grinning. "Well," he said, "we were both at the lake on one of those really hot days we had, and I swam out to this raft in the middle, and there he was, doing gorgeous dives, and I like swooned."

"Literally or figuratively?"

Terry wobbled, balancing on one foot. "I wanted to literally, because then he'd have had to rescue me, but no, only figuratively."

"And?"

"And what?"

"And then what happened?"

"And then we just sat there talking after he came up from a dive and I told him how beautiful he—I mean *it*, you know, the dive—was. See, I'm not shy. Not like some people who just stare and stutter."

Jamie punched him lightly. "That's not fair."

"Yeah, I know. Sorry."

"So?"

"So we started talking and stuff, and we decided to meet at the lake the next day, and the next and the next—and now my folks are beginning to get suspicious. I'm thinking of telling them, you know, coming out to them."

Jamie realized she was staring at him. "You really must be sure," she said after a moment. "Probably a Probably, I'd say."

"Yep. Probably a Probably."

"Wow, Terry. It must feel good, you know, to be that sure." He nodded.

"What about whoever-he-is? Does he love you back? Does he know you love him?"

Terry jumped down off the wall. "That's the problem. Mucho biggo problemo. He's a Maybe, too, only he's freaked about it. I mean really freaked, more than you and I ever were, even in our most freaked moments. He says his folks'll make him leave home if they find out, and he's got this whole religion thing, like God doesn't like gays, and being gay is immoral, and you'll fry in hell if you're gay. He even read Bible verses to me one night, and I tried to tell him that what the

Bible says about homosexuality is as outdated as what it says about women and dietary laws and stuff, but that didn't help."

"Have you . . . ? You know."

"No. I kissed him once and he cried."

"Geeze."

"Yeah. That doesn't exactly fill me with confidence. But he's so sweet, Jamie, and he says he does love me. And it's okay with me if we're, you know, platonic. Just being with him's— well, special." Terry looked off toward the harbor. "Really, really special," he repeated softly, as if to himself.

Jamie waited, but Terry didn't seem to be going to say any more. "So," she asked cautiously, "so, who is he?"

"Ernie Rivers."

"Ernie Rivers!" Jamie exclaimed. "Only the star of the swim team, right?"

"Right. That's another reason why he's so freaked about us. Me and him, I mean. Can you imagine what'd happen on the team if anyone found out?" Terry grimaced. "But you'd better believe you'll be getting great coverage of swimming this year."

"Fine. Just don't stint on the other stuff. If we start running swimming instead of football, it'll be the end of the paper."

"Yeah, yeah, I know. The end of me, too, if jerks like Brandon and Al catch on." Terry started walking again.

Jamie caught up with him and put her hand on his arm. "Hey," she said softly. "Terry. I really am happy for you." She stood on her toes and gave him a quick kiss on the cheek. "Really happy. You let me know if there's anything I can do, okay?"

"Do?"

Jamie shrugged. "Be around when you tell your folks. Or

afterward." She paused. "At least I could tell Ernie I'm a Maybe. Or you could tell him."

Terry turned toward her, almost shyly. "I'd like to tell him that. And then we could all, you know, do stuff together sometimes. It'll look less obvious if you're with us. It might make Ernie feel—I don't know. Less pressured?"

"Okay," Jamie said, although she wasn't sure she'd enjoy being the third member of a threesome. "How about this weekend? We could all go to the movies or something." She stopped; they were at the corner of her street, Willow Road.

"Sure! I'll ask Ernie. That'd be great." Terry shifted his book bag. "See you," he said. "Dream of you-know-who."

"Oh, shove it," Jamie called after him good-naturedly. "*You* dream of you-know-who!"

She turned down her street, wondering if she envied him. Perhaps not, she decided; maybe it's better to be a Maybe, with all possibilities still open. Then she stopped, mildly curious, at the next corner, where a red cardboard sign with machine-printed white letters stared at her from its wooden post:

LISA BUEL FOR SCHOOL COMMITTEE

Several more signs greeted her as she walked toward home, and then she saw why: a Ford pickup truck was making its way slowly along the road, stopping every few hundred yards to put up another sign.

By morning, there were Lisa Buel signs all over Wilson.

T W O

"There's a vacancy on the school committee," Jamie's mother said at breakfast when Jamie mentioned the signs. "Remember my talking about Mrs. Cochran? Her husband got a new job in August and they moved to New Jersey. Lisa Buel is—how can I put it? She moved to Wilson about five years ago and went to school committee meetings all last year. She's very conservative, and she argued against the new health ed curriculum, specifically the parts that have to do with sex; she claims sex education encourages immorality. In fact, she's spent a lot of time trying to convince people to object to the curriculum on moral grounds. I think she's been pretty successful." Mrs. Crawford took a swallow of coffee, then got up from the table. "Thank goodness Anna Pembar's running for school committee, too."

"Nomi's mom?" Jamie asked, surprised. "Why, for heaven's sake?"

"Why not?" Mrs. Crawford opened the door to the back stairs and yelled, "Ronnie! Rise and shine!" Then she returned to the table. Sunlight played over her features, small and even like Jamie's, but with tiny smile wrinkles at the corners of her eyes and mouth. "Anna Pembar's conservative, too, but she's also reasonable, a lot more reasonable than Lisa Buel. If Lisa gets in, I'll think seriously about early retirement." Mrs. Crawford took another swallow of coffee. "A lot of people would say Lisa's a pillar of the community, but—well, remember Mr. Bergemot, who used to teach sixth grade?"

"The guy who left last year?"

"The very one. He left because Lisa Buel saw him a couple of times with a woman who wasn't his wife, and she started a move to get him fired as 'an unfit role model.' I think that's what she called it."

Jamie put down her own coffee mug. "But he was divorced, wasn't he?"

"No, separated. Lisa thought it was immoral for him to see another woman while he was still technically married. The school committee refused to fire him, but she and a few others made his life so miserable he resigned." Mrs. Crawford looked at her watch. "We've got some lazy men in this family," she said, getting up. "There are already people on this year's school committee who oppose nearly everything that's halfway innovative. Lisa Buel just might give them the courage to force things to go their way." She went to the stairs again. "Ronnie! Dick, you too!" She sighed. "Your dad's as bad as your brother. Slugabeds, both of them. More coffee? More cereal?"

"Nope. You wouldn't really take early retirement, would you? You'd go crazy if you stopped teaching, and then we'd go crazy watching you go crazy, and the entire family would fall apart."

"No, I probably wouldn't retire." Jamie's mother poured herself more coffee. "But it'd be hard not to. Last summer Lisa kept telling us—the health ed curriculum committee—that it wasn't any of our business as teachers to even broach the subject of sex education. When we explained that lots of parents don't talk about sex at all with their kids, she got angry and said that should show us even more that it isn't any of our business, that we're interfering with parents' rights."

Jamie gave a short laugh. "She'll love my editorial this week, then. And speaking of that, I've got to get going." She pushed her chair back.

"Oh? What editorial?"

There was a clatter on the stairs, and Jamie's nine-year-old brother Ronnie burst into the room, toothpaste smeared on his mouth and a Red Sox T-shirt on backwards. He was followed closely by their father, buttoning his old blue flannel shirt and rubbing his eyes. One reason, Dad had always said, why he owned and managed the town's only hardware store was that there was no way he could keep fisherman's hours. Ronnie took after him.

Jamie crammed the last spoonful of corn flakes into her mouth and gulped down the rest of her coffee. "Tell you later. Morning, Dad. Ron, is it cool to wear backwards shirts these days? 'Bye, Mom."

And she was out the door.

Later, after school, Jamie worked on her editorial again, closeted in the newspaper office with Terry, who at her request was polishing a story a new reporter had written about the prospects of the school's football team, the Wilson Wolves. The sounds of departing students made a distant hum punctuated by shouts and clanging locker doors; a fly, buzzing loudly at the window, occasionally masked the muffled tapping of Terry's electronic typewriter and Jamie's computer keyboard.

In an hour or so, Jamie heard the rasp of paper being ripped out of the typewriter, and Terry thrust the football story at her. "Here you are, Madame Editor. Great head, right?"

Jamie glanced at the yellow copy paper:

WILSON WILL WIN, WISH WOLVES

She groaned. "Wish? That's a pretty weak verb, Terry."

"Yeah, but what else is there that begins with W? Besides whine?"

"I don't know, but you'll come up with something." She handed the paper back to him.

"By deadline? I'm not so sure."

"You've got till Thursday, for Pete's sake."

"Yeah, but I've got two practices to cover, plus a track meet, and not enough reporters."

"You'll manage." Jamie returned to her editorial.

"You're hard, Jamie, you're hard."

"Darn right."

"How about 'Wilson Will Win, Say Wolves'?" Terry asked.

"Sure. Still catchy, and it's a lot stronger." Jamie held out her hand for the paper again, penciled in the change, and scanned the rest of the story, nodding. "Good, Terry. A tad long . . ."

"No," said Terry. "No, no, no, no, and no! This is the first issue of the year, and the first football story of the year, and the time when the jocks, bless 'em, are trying to stir up that elusive quality known as, er, school spirit—remember? There is no way you're going to bury it on page forty-seven below the fold in three-point type. No way! Besides, you asked me to get this story, remember? And the guy who wrote it is really proud of it."

"Okay, okay. We don't even," Jamie added as the office door opened, "have a page forty-seven."

"Page four, then. Whatever. Hi, Ernie." Terry smiled at the slender blond boy who'd just come in, and Jamie looked up quickly. Ernie Rivers had always had the reputation of being a shy, quiet, academic loner, but he'd gained the other students' notice and respect when he'd started swimming and diving. As far as Jamie knew, he'd always been friendly to everyone but close to no one.

"Hi, Terry," Ernie said with a shy smile that Jamie could see was just for him. But despite the smile, he seemed ill at ease. "And hi, Jamie." He glanced around the small, narrow office. "Nice," he said. "Crowded, but nice."

"Hi, Ernie," Jamie said. "Welcome to chaos." Trying to see the office through Ernie's eyes, she scanned the two battered green file cabinets with old issues piled on top of them; the scratched layout table strewn with scissors, X-ACTO knives, and rubber cement jars; her desk and Matt's, with scraps of paper, pens, a dictionary or two, and photos waiting for captions scattered around their computers; the long table where the reporters occasionally worked, lined with old typewriters and edged with uncomfortable stools. "It's crowded, but it's home." She stood up. "Hey, I hear maybe I'm going to the movies with you guys this weekend. Or didn't . . ."

Ernie's smile tensed a little. "Terry told me. Sounds good."

"Of course," said Terry, sitting on one of the stools, "there aren't any good movies except all the way down in George-port . . ."

"That's only an hour away," Jamie pointed out.

"Right," said Terry. "I'll drive. Okay, Ernie?"

"Sure. Um, listen, Terry, why I really came in was to tell you when that meet's scheduled for. It'll be October ninth."

"Thanks." Terry flipped a page on the huge calendar that was tacked to the office wall and wrote SWIM MEET in large letters in the square for October 9. It was, Jamie saw, a Saturday.

"That's a four-schools meet," Terry explained to Jamie. "We've got to cover it."

"You're the sports editor. Go for it." She turned to Ernie. "You guys going to win?"

"We're sure going to try. Terry . . . ?"

"Yes. Story's okay, right?" Terry said to Jamie.

She glanced at it again, changed a couple of commas, and nodded.

Terry gathered up books and pens, switched off his typewriter, gave Jamie a perfunctory wave, and left with Ernie. Their shoulders touched, then moved quickly apart.

Jamie stayed in the office for a while after finishing her editorial, hoping Nomi would drop in with the op-ed piece she'd more or less indicated she'd do. Cindy came with a few more ads, followed by one or two reporters, and then Jack arrived with his storm interview. But by 4:30, when there was no sign of Nomi, Jamie gave up. She closed the office and walked

through town, past more LISA BUEL FOR SCHOOL COMMIT-
TEE signs, about four of them to every homemade-looking
one for Anna Pembar. It had been an unseasonably warm afternoon, and the slowly descending sun glowed lazily on the
white clapboards of the general store, the pharmacy, the souvenir shop, the bookstore. Jamie walked through town and
along the narrow causeway road leading to the working harbor. Gold-green marsh grass waved gently on one side, and
herring gulls dipped and mewed around one or two returning
boats on the other.

Jamie slipped off her sweater, tied it around her waist, and
went out on Cal Pembar's dock, where Nomi's dad was stacking lobster traps.

"Jamie, my girl!" Mr. Pembar said cheerfully, his bronzed,
weather-beaten face crinkling with his smile. "Haven't seen
much of you lately. And Nomi was a real thundercloud last
night. You and she have a tiff?"

"Sort of," Jamie admitted. "But it'll heal, I think."

Mr. Pembar laughed. "Lordy," he said, "I remember when
you two were no bigger'n a couple of minutes and you had a
fight over a teddy bear. Took you two days to make up, and
Nomi's mother and I thought she'd never stop crying."

"I remember," said Jamie, hoping their present quarrel
would turn out to be that simple.

Mr. Pembar tossed an undersize lobster over the side.
"Missed this fella," he said as if to himself. "Well," he went on
to Jamie, "just so the two of you don't cry for days over whatever this fight's about."

"We won't." Jamie turned to go, then stopped. "Good luck
to Mrs. Pembar. I hope she gets on the school committee. So
does Mom."

"And so do I. At least I think I do. I don't much hold with some of that Buel woman's ideas. But it's a hard job, and it'll only get harder this year, what with that new program to worry about. And then come March and the regular school committee election, Anna'll have to campaign all over again if she still wants the job. There'll probably be another big fuss then about the new program."

"Yes, I guess there might be." Jamie suddenly found herself wondering just what Mr. Pembar thought about "the new program," but before she could sound him out, he'd already returned to his traps—and then Jamie spotted a tall figure, camera bag and fancy Nikon slung over her shoulder, walking along the causeway road.

"See you later, Mr. Pembar," Jamie said quickly, and ran along the dock. "Tess!" she called.

Tessa turned, her star-chain earrings and the star in her nose sparkling against her dark skin. Then she stopped, a quizzical half smile on her lips.

"Hi," Jamie said breathlessly when she reached her.

"Hi."

Suddenly Jamie had no idea what to say. "Um," she finally managed, "looking for pictures for the paper?"

Tessa nodded.

"How's it going?"

"Okay," Tessa said noncommittally, shifting her camera bag. "I don't think I've ever seen so many boats."

"Yeah, we've got a lot. I mean, half the town's population fishes for a living, so we've kind of got to. Lots of little kids learn to row before they learn to ride bikes." She stopped, afraid she was chattering mindlessly.

"Did you?"

"Huh?"

Tessa looked down at her; Jamie realized Tessa was at least an inch taller. "Did you learn to row before you learned to ride a bike?"

"I—well, no. My dad's in hardware, not fishing, so I learned to ride a bike first."

Tessa's smile broadened a little. "Good. So did I, actually. That means we've got something in common."

Jamie laughed self-consciously. "Yeah." She fell into step beside Tessa as the taller girl strode toward town along the narrow road. "Yeah, I guess maybe it does. We've got the newspaper in common, too, or we probably will. You don't have much competition for the photo editor's job. Only two other sets of photos came in, and . . ."

"Any good?"

"What? Oh, I don't know. Matt won't let us look at them till they're all in. But I know who submitted them, and I know what the photos you showed us look like."

There was an awkward pause, during which Jamie struggled to think of something—anything—to say.

"What's that church?" Tessa asked finally, pointing to a small white steeple just visible above the trees ahead.

"Lord's Assembly. My friend Nomi, you know, the art editor, goes there." She pointed to the right. "There's also a Congregational church, but you can't see it from here."

Tessa nodded. "I shot both of them. I think a town's churches kind of symbolize the town. You know, the people in it. We don't go anywhere here yet. But my mother's looking into it."

"There's a Catholic church, too," Jamie told her. "Saint

Joseph's. It's up on the hill, sort of between the interstate and the town center. And there's a Methodist church in the next town, and a synagogue down in Georgeport, and . . ." She realized she was chattering again, but Tessa spoke before Jamie's voice trailed off in embarrassed silence.

"I'd rather go to church in the woods. Or"—Tessa swept her hand around the way she had in the newspaper office—"or by the water, with the seagulls and those little skittery birds . . ."

"Sandpipers, probably."

"Sandpipers. And the fishes and the bugs and the waves. I'm a pagan, I guess. A pagan-Catholic-Quaker-Unitarian-witch. I think God likes the outdoors best, don't you? I mean, that's what God created; it was people made the buildings, even the churches."

Jamie felt her tension ease. "You're right. I never quite thought of it that way, but—yeah, you're right. Sometimes when I've got a problem or something, I just go down to Sloan's Beach. That's on the other side of where we are now, beyond where the yachts are. You saw that harbor, right?"

"And took pictures there."

"Great! I go down there and walk, or I sit on the rocks and watch the ocean. It makes me feel"—she hesitated—"makes me feel little, sort of, and that nothing that bothers me can be all that bad. It makes me know the world's going to go on forever, with me or without me." Shut up, Jamie, she ordered herself. Why would Tessa care?

But Tessa didn't seem to mind. "It'll go on forever if we don't blow it up first, or choke it to death." She pointed at a huge house just visible among trees and bushes at the point where the causeway road widened. "I tried to shoot that place, too, but I don't think the house'll show through the shrub-bery. Who lives there, anyway?"

Jamie smiled; everyone who was new in town asked that question sooner or later. "Mom calls him 'the laird of Wil-son,' you know, like some Scottish nobleman. His name is Philbert Davenport . . ."

"His name is WHAT?"

Jamie's smile became a grin. "Philbert Davenport."

Tessa looked as if she was about to burst out laughing. "Like the nut and the sofa, right?"

Jamie did laugh. "Right. And he's richer than anyone in the world, practically, has a couple of yachts, one of which has a helicopter and a Volkswagen Beetle on its afterdeck, and his grandfather used to own half the town. The family still owns five or six huge fish-packing plants."

"Ugh. Smelly." Tessa wrinkled her nose, which made the tiny star more noticeable. Jamie found herself staring at it, fascinated, then looked away self-consciously.

"Right. Very smelly. And there've been rumors that Philbert's got a drug-running operation. Every time I hear a boat at night, I wonder, and so does everyone else in town, in-cluding the coast guard. But no one's been able to prove any-thing."

"What does Philbert look like?"

"No one's seen him for years. He's a recluse."

"So who uses the yacht and the helicopter and the Volkswa-gen?" Tessa had unslung her Nikon and was fishing in her camera bag, from which she produced a long telephoto lens. "Here." She unscrewed the Nikon's short lens and handed it to Jamie; purple, Jamie decided, studying Tessa's nail polish. But underneath the odd trappings, Tessa seemed—well, not quite like everyone else, but not as different from them as she looked.

"I don't know who uses them," Jamie said, answering Tessa's question. "Maybe they're just for show."

"Or," said Tessa, deftly attaching the long lens, "maybe they're fake. Just stage props, to impress everyone." Balancing the lens with one hand, she lifted the camera to her eye. "Hey," she said, after twisting the lens back and forth a few times. "There's someone outside the house in a wheelchair. Maybe it's Philbert." She handed the camera to Jamie.

Jamie took it, surprised at how clumsy it was with the long lens weighing it down in front, and squinted through the eyepiece. She could just make out a wheelchair, or what could have been a wheelchair, and a splash of white—a blanket, perhaps—with a triangular patch of brighter white above it.

"I think it's his beard," said Tessa.

After a moment, Jamie realized that Tessa meant the triangular patch. "I bet you're right." She handed the camera back.

"So that's what Philbert looks like," said Tessa. "Two white blobs, a blanket blob and a triangle-beard blob. So much for money."

Jamie laughed again. "Yeah," she said. "Right."

There was another silence, less awkward this time, and they walked on.

Not long after they reached the main road, but before the houses thickened as the road approached the town center, Tessa stopped, pointing to a side street. "I go left here."

"Robert Road."

Tessa nodded. "Thanks for the tour."

"It really wasn't one."

"No, it wasn't, but that seemed the right thing to say. I mean, like it's your town."

"Wrong," Jamie said emphatically. "It's everyone's town who lives here."

Then, as Tessa waved and walked away, she thought of what her mother had said about Lisa Buel, and wondered.

THREE

After supper, Jamie went up to her room to tackle her math homework, but found her mind drifting to Tessa and then to Terry and Ernie. "A Maybe Probably," she muttered, twisting her pencil between her thumb and forefinger. "No, a Probably Probably. So what am I?" She gazed out her window at the working harbor, watching the lights and trying to keep her mind blank. But soon she gave up and tried again to work. After a few unsuccessful minutes, her eyes strayed to the corner of her desk and her copy of the press release announcing the new health education curriculum:

> Homosexuality is to be integrated into lifestyle discussions at all grade levels. Books dealing with gay families should be available in primary and elementary libraries, along with books dealing with mixed-race and other minority families. English and social studies teachers in middle school and high school should acknowledge the sexual orientation, if relevant, of authors, political figures, athletes, etc., just as they acknowledge the gender

and the racial and ethnic backgrounds of such people. Gay relationships should be acknowledged in sex education classes in a nonjudgmental way at all levels when relationships are discussed. The purpose of this curriculum is not to encourage any particular lifestyle or behavior but rather to reflect the world as it is, so our students can better understand it.

"I wish them luck" is what Jamie's father had said when her mother had brought that statement home from a committee meeting during the summer.

"Gross!" was Ronnie's comment; Mrs. Crawford had shushed him promptly.

And Jamie had sat there silently at the dinner table, a sudden lump in her throat, fighting tears, for where had that curriculum been back when she and Terry were in elementary school, being teased, or in middle school, and wondering?

"Too little, too late," she muttered now, going to her closet and rooting in its back corner for the small locked strongbox she'd kept there for several years in which she filed newspaper clippings about gay people and issues, state laws and city ordinances, photos of events like Gay Pride Day parades, plus a list of books and an old yellow notebook—a diary she'd kept sporadically since eighth grade. She closed the door to her room, unlocked the strongbox, and flipped through some of the diary's entries:

Who am I? What am I? How can I go on not knowing? . . .

I feel like I'm going to burst; Sally Lawrence smiled at me! . . .

Terry says he dreamed a boy was kissing him. God, if I could only dream that Sally was kissing me! . . .

Sally's got a boyfriend. I think I'm going to die . . .

I feel so weird. I feel so alone. If it weren't for Terry, I think I'd want to kill myself. Everyone assumes everyone is straight. WHERE ARE THE PEOPLE LIKE US *who aren't sure, who might not be straight? I know they're somewhere; sometimes gay people are in books or on TV or in the movies—but there sure don't seem to be any in Wilson* . . .

I wish I could meet a girl who isn't boy crazy. Then maybe I could know. (But maybe I really do know?) I wish some gorgeous girl would move to Wilson and like me. No—she doesn't have to be gorgeous, just nice. My arms feel like they want to hug someone, and I hug Terry and my parents and sometimes even my brother, and Nomi, too, and that's nice, but it's not the same. Terry's body's so hard when I hug him; his chest is stiff and hard. So's Dad's. I know I'd rather hug a girl; heck, I'd rather hug Mom or Nomi; they're more—comfortable, I guess would be the word, maybe. Well, more than that, too; sometimes I wonder what I want when I hug Nomi, but anyway, we don't hug much. But it's not only that. I want someone who's more than a friend, someone who's always there for me, someone who I can tell anything to, someone who I can hold and who'll hold me, who . . . *I'd better stop* . . .

I saw a girl today on the beach who must have come off one of the yachts or something. She was golden; her bathing suit was yellow and she had this neat tan and her hair was long and blond and she smiled at me! I smiled back, and I was going to try to go

over and talk to her, but then this boy came along and she smiled at
him, more like she meant it than when she'd smiled at me, and he
sat down next to her. Lucky guy! . . .

I feel like I'm floating, waiting for my real life to happen,
waiting to meet myself. Sometimes I don't care if I'm straight or
gay; I just want to know. Sometimes—a lot of the time—I'm scared
of being gay. What will happen to me? What will Mom and Dad
and Ronnie say? Will newspapers hire me? Can I be fired if they
find out? Will I get AIDS? Is it evil to be gay? Does God really
hate gay people? I want to find someone to live with, like we were
married, but is that possible? The books I've read seem to say it is,
but they're books; maybe they're not true. And I know there are
laws against gay people marrying. But I read a newspaper article
about two lesbians adopting a baby; is that really possible? A baby
would be nice . . .

Maybe there's something terribly wrong with me, something
that doesn't have anything to do with being gay . . .

Jamie closed her yellow notebook. Then she opened it
again and, hesitantly, wrote:

I've met someone. I've met someone I think I could really like.
Terry's met someone, too, so maybe I'm just saying I could really
like the girl I've met because I'm jealous. I don't think so, though. I
know I'm scared. Suppose I really like this girl and she's straight? I
mean, she must be straight; most everyone is. I should ignore her.
But I think she's going to be photo editor, so I can't ignore her.
God, I wish I'd never met her! I wish she hadn't come to
Wilson . . .

But that's not true, Jamie thought, locking the notebook in the box again and returning it to her closet. She'd never been sure if her mother had found the box or not, cleaning; if she had, she hadn't said anything. Sometimes Jamie almost wished her mother would find it, so they could talk about it, but most of the time she was glad she probably hadn't.

What will happen, Jamie wondered, when Terry tells his parents?

What would happen if I told mine?

Early Thursday morning, deadline time, there was a manila envelope of photos but no op-ed piece in the newspaper's mailbox, so Jamie waited for Nomi on the school steps before first period, forcing herself not to open the envelope. There was no indication on it of who'd submitted it, but Jamie was pretty sure it was from Tessa.

Brandon Tomkins and Al Checkers sauntered across the student parking lot. Sam Mills, a sophomore who had gravitated to Brandon the way iron gravitates to a magnet, followed in their wake.

Brandon's head was almost devoid of hair, Jamie noticed, the word "skinhead" popping into her mind; he must have had it shaved during the summer. As usual, his slack lips gave his face a sullen, hungry look, and his biceps, showing below the sleeves of his T-shirt, bulged and rippled even more than they had last year. Brandon was captain of the wrestling team; he and Al worked out as religiously as kids like Ernie studied.

Al, shorter and thicker than Brandon, didn't seem to have changed at all over the summer. He still dressed neatly in chinos instead of jeans, and his usual light-blue Oxford shirt was stiffly pressed. He was handsome in a rugged, angular way, and his posture was as erect and military as Brandon's was slouched and indolent.

As Jamie watched Brandon and Sam stub out cigarettes as they crossed the driveway to the steps just ahead of a group of nervous-looking freshmen, it was clearer than ever to her that Sam was modeling himself after the other two. He dressed like Al, although he was chubby instead of stocky, and his head was shaved like Brandon's. He walked like Brandon, too, Jamie realized as he sauntered up to his girlfriend, Karen Hodges, a pretty sophomore with light brown braids, and put his arm possessively around her.

"Hey, butch," Brandon called to Jamie, "getting any?"

Karen giggled.

Jamie ignored the comment, as she always did now, though as usual she felt it stab inside.

Senior class beauty Vicky Chase met Brandon and his friends at the school door with a kiss and a toss of her pale blond hair. Then she looked beyond him and smiled, giving a little finger wave; Jamie, suddenly realizing the wave was meant for her, waved back.

She had always liked Vicky, though some girls didn't almost on principle, since boys flocked to Vicky whether she wanted them to or not. Mostly, it was clear, she did want them to, but despite expectations to the contrary, Jamie knew Vicky'd never stolen another girl's boyfriend and probably never would. "Poor Vicky," Jamie's mother had commented when, hours after a junior high dance, several older boys had gone to Vicky's house and shouted her name repeatedly, waking her parents and mortifying her. "It's not always wonderful to be beautiful," Mrs. Crawford had said. Even though now it was obvious that Vicky could take care of herself with men, Jamie had never forgotten that.

Now, as Cindy and Jack came up to Jamie, Vicky called out, "I'm really looking forward to the paper this year, you guys!"

"Thanks," Jamie called back, and Cindy and Jack waved.

"Is Nomi doing that op-ed?" Cindy asked, turning to Jamie, and when Jamie said, "I sure hope so," Cindy answered, "I almost wish I could write it, but it'd be quite a stretch. I'm glad about the condoms—we both are, right, Jack?"

"Right," Jack said emphatically. "Trouble with getting that op-ed is that most kids are for it, the condoms, I mean. I'll ask around, though, in case Nomi doesn't come through. Okay?"

"Sure," Jamie answered as Cindy pulled Jack to the door. "Thanks."

Terry ran up the steps soon after Cindy and Jack went in, stopped for a second, and quipped, "Waiting for the bus?" As he ducked inside, Jamie spotted Nomi's boyfriend's car rounding the corner, heading for the student parking lot. Jamie had always liked Clark Alman, who occasionally wrote for the paper. Last year he'd contributed several profiles of teachers who'd done interesting things, like the math teacher who'd written a novel and the French teacher who'd spent a summer sailing along the Eastern U.S. coast. Clark was head of the youth group at Lord's Assembly Church; Nomi had started dating him soon after she'd joined the group last year. Al Checkers had joined then, too, much to everyone's surprise— even, apparently, Brandon's, for Brandon had made some heavy-handed jokes about "getting religion" that rumor had it had almost cost him Al's friendship. Not quite, though, Jamie had observed with disappointment, feeling that Brandon and Al would lose some of their power if they were no longer able to egg each other on.

In a few minutes, Nomi and Clark came toward her, Clark

with his arm lightly across Nomi's shoulders and Nomi snuggled under it. They walked together fluidly, as if they shared the same body.

Could I walk like that with a girl—with Tessa—Jamie caught herself wondering as she ran down the steps to meet them.

"Hey, guys," she called as casually as she could. "Deadline day, Nom'. Got an op-ed for me?"

Nomi glanced at Clark, then brushed back her soft red hair with her free hand. "No, Jamie, I—no, I don't. I'm sorry. I thought about it, but I'm no good at writing. And anyway," she went on, as if embarrassed, "Mom's had me listening to her campaign speech for school committee, and I'm working on this really big painting, and I'm way behind in the social studies reading, and I just . . ."

"What Nomi's saying," Clark explained, his brown eyes twinkling, "is that she doesn't have an op-ed."

Jamie tried to disguise her disappointment. "If you keep it short, Nom', I can wait till lunchtime."

"No, no, Jamie, thanks."

Jamie put her hand on Nomi's arm. "I'll help you if you want. I could look it over when you've done it, or we could talk it through." She paused; Nomi looked very uncomfortable. "Matt was right, Nomi," she said gently. "We should represent both sides."

"I know, Jamie, but . . . I even asked Clark if he'd write it."

"But I've got this killer of a chem assignment, and I just didn't have time. If I'd known earlier . . ."

Jamie turned to him, giving up on Nomi. "It'd be perfect for you, Clark. Look, how about I let you have till first thing tomorrow? We're having to hold space for a piece about the school committee meeting tonight anyway; maybe the print shop people will be willing to wait till tomorrow for the op-ed, too."

"No good," said Clark.

"Oh, come on, guys; maybe you could even write the op-ed together, at lunch or something. Please? Please with sugar? Whipped cream? Strawberries?"

Clark laughed and Nomi smiled, but they both shook their heads.

And then the bell rang, sending them all inside.

During the day, Jamie asked several other people if they'd write an op-ed against the nurse's handing out condoms, but just about everyone she spoke to was on the pro side. The others said they didn't have time or didn't want to air their views in public. Right before last period, Jack told her he'd had the same experience.

After school in the newspaper office, Jamie handed Matt her editorial; he scanned it, nodding as he read. "Good piece," he said, giving it back to her. "Now you've got an op-ed, right, Nomi?"

Nomi looked up from the layout table where she was working on the last of Cindy's ads. "No, I didn't do it."

"How come?"

"I—I can't write, Matt. I'm an artist, not a writer. And I didn't really say I'd do it." She turned to Jamie. "Did I?"

"No," Jamie said. "I guess you didn't. But . . ."

Matt glanced at Jamie, then said, "You don't have to be all that eloquent to write an op-ed. We really do need something to balance Jamie's point of view."

"I've already tried unsuccessfully to get someone else,"

Jamie said. "And so has Jack. But maybe I could add a request at the end of the editorial, inviting kids to submit op-eds for next week's paper. I guess since this is the first issue, we could reprint the welcome page from the school handbook to fill the space we've been saving for the op-ed."

"Good idea." Matt handed her editorial back to her as Terry came in and sat down quietly next to Nomi. "Do it. Just put a line or two in italics at the end of your editorial asking for other opinions; don't weaken your ending. Now—is there anything else I haven't seen yet? Stories from staff reporters? Ads?"

"Nope," said Jamie. "You've seen it all. We just have to leave space for my report of the school committee candidates' night tonight. We can go ahead and take everything else to the print shop and drop off the school committee piece early tomorrow morning. Let me just write that op-ed request." She scrawled a couple of lines at the bottom of her editorial and handed it to Matt.

"Nice," Matt said, after reading it, so Jamie added the lines on her computer, printed out the final piece, and handed it to Nomi. "That'll do the trick, I think," Matt went on. "At least it'll show we want to represent the other side. Okay— let's have a look at the photo applications. We're going to need a picture of the school committee candidates, and we might as well ask whoever gets the job to go tonight and take it."

Jamie reached for the three blank manila envelopes on the back of her desk; she'd purposely shuffled them around so she couldn't tell anymore which one was Tessa's. Terry and Nomi moved a little aside as Jamie spread the photos out in three rows on the layout table.

Matt gave a low whistle. "There's no doubt. No doubt at all." He pointed to the middle row of pictures. "These are absolutely the best. At least in my opinion. Jamie?"

Please let them be Tessa's, Jamie prayed silently. Aloud, while Nomi and Terry murmured agreement, she said, "Yeah, you're right."

The photos in the middle were the sharpest and clearest, but more than that, they showed a fine sense of composition, and something potentially newsworthy was happening in each one. There was Lord's Assembly Church, but not just the church: a small girl was sitting tearfully on the steps, clutching a broken doll. Next was the working harbor, as background to a close-up of a lobster boat, unloading. The last photo showed the souvenir shop in the center of town, with a huge RV in front of it. A middle-aged male tourist was bending down beside it, examining a tire.

Matt turned over the RV photo. "I guess you can go find that new girl, Jamie. Tessa—what's her last name?"

"Gillespie."

"Right. Tell her she's got the job and ask her if she can go tonight."

Terry gave Jamie a shamelessly obvious wink, which Jamie did her best to ignore.

"I think I saw her up in the art room," said Nomi. "Want me to tell her? It's my mom she's going to be photographing tonight."

"I thought you didn't like her," Jamie said. "Tessa, I mean. You weren't overly friendly when she came in."

"She's a good photographer. I didn't *not* like her. She just seemed sort of stuck-up. And it takes a bit to get used to her looking so flamboyant."

"She's not stuck-up," Jamie said angrily. Almost immediately, she felt her face redden. "I'll go with you."

"Which leaves me," said Terry with a long-suffering sigh, "to take the paper to the print shop. You owe me, guys."

Tessa was sitting near a window in a far corner of the art room, her hair backlit by the fading afternoon sun. She seemed very absorbed in what she was doing—cutting, Jamie saw as she and Nomi approached, parts of photos from larger ones and positioning them carefully on a piece of white oaktag.

"Hi, Tessa," Nomi said, sounding perfectly friendly. She peered over Tessa's shoulder. "What're you making?"

Tessa glanced from Nomi to Jamie and back again. "Just a photo collage. I put bits of old pictures together and then photograph them so they become one picture. This one's old family photos, for my great-grandmother. What's up?"

"You got the job," Jamie told her. "Congratulations. You're the new photo editor of the Wilson High *Telegraph*." She studied the collage, an artfully arranged collection of pictures of men, women, babies, children, pets, and houses, spanning, Jamie could tell from the clothes, several generations and eras. Some of the photos were black-and-white faded to brown, some were clear black-and-white, and the most recent were in color, but somehow Tessa had made them all fit together, using the color to offset the black-and-white and brown ones, and vice versa. "That's really great," Jamie said, then thought how dumb that sounded—inadequate.

"Thanks. And"—Tessa chuckled, her eyes shining—"thanks for the job."

"Don't thank us," Nomi said politely. "You earned it. Your photos were the best. And this is even better." She pointed to the collage.

"Yeah," Tessa said, "it is, or it's going to be, but will my great-grandma like it? That's the real question. She's kind of hard to please, and it's her ninety-eighth birthday present . . ."

"Wow!" Jamie eased herself onto a stool next to Tessa's drawing board. "I never knew anyone that old."

"Neither did I." Tessa smiled. "Each year that's what I tell her. 'Great-grandma, I never knew anyone as old as you,' and each year she tells me she never did either, and we both laugh. She's my favorite lady."

"I never even knew my grandmothers," Jamie said enviously, "let alone my great-grandmothers. One of my grandmothers died when I was seven and the other one died before I was born. So did both my grandfathers."

Tessa flashed Jamie a sympathetic look. "I'm sorry. It's good to have old people around. Some kids don't like them, but I think they're special. Lots of them are, anyway."

Nomi shuffled her feet, and Jamie suddenly realized she was still there. "Yeah," Nomi said awkwardly. "My grandfather? He's in a nursing home, but he's really sharp. Lots of the people there aren't, though, you know what I mean? It's like they're not in their bodies anymore, and their minds don't work. Some of them can't think beyond the moment and others can't seem to catch up *to* the moment. It's sad. Hey," she went on, "I hate to break this up, but I've got to go." She poked Jamie as if she expected Jamie to say something, but Jamie had no idea what. "Tonight?" Nomi prompted her. "School committee?"

"Oh, right! I forgot." She explained to Tessa about the special election. "So tonight the two candidates," she went on, "get to make speeches to anyone who wants to listen. I'm doing the story and we'll need a photo to go with it."

"And," said Tessa, putting down her scissors, "you'd like your new photo editor to take it. Sure. What time?"

FOUR

Lisa Buel, tall and self-possessed, with an angular but not un-attractive face, smiled warmly at her audience that evening from the stage of the school auditorium. "I think you'll all agree," she said, "that it's definitely time for a change, for a re-turn to traditional values. Now, I'm not sure that anyone here in Wilson, except perhaps for a few misguided but still good souls, has seriously departed from the values we all cherish. But I do feel we need to put the brakes on here and there, and be vigilant. It's our children, after all, who are at stake, our most precious and most impressionable assets. I think we need to re-examine our priorities, and if I'm elected, I'll try to help do that. Thank you."

Tessa, who'd been squatting in the aisle in her red cape, snapped Mrs. Buel's picture as she sat down to an enthusiastic round of applause. It was louder and longer, Jamie realized, scribbling on her notepad, than the applause Nomi's mother had gotten a few minutes earlier.

The moderator called for questions, and Jamie was startled to hear her own mother's voice. "Just where would you put on the brakes, Lisa?" Mrs. Crawford asked.

Mrs. Buel stood up again. "Why, I'm not sure of the specifics yet, Margaret," she answered pleasantly. "I just think we need to take a long, careful look at a number of issues."

"Curricular issues? As I recall, you have some objections to the new health curriculum." There was an angry edge to Mrs. Crawford's voice.

"That's right," Mrs. Buel said smoothly. "I do feel we need to take another look at that. At all issues, really."

Out of the corner of her eye, Jamie saw her mother's mouth tense.

"I don't trust her," Mrs. Crawford said angrily at home after the meeting, slamming the cocoa box down on the kitchen table, where Jamie and her father sat; Ronnie was in the living room, watching TV. "Do you realize—you must, Jamie; you're a word person—that she didn't say anything specific in her speech? And yet she sure was specific to the curriculum committee last summer, and I know she's been talking to the people she's gotten to support her. But she's waiting till she's elected before she comes out in the open to the town at large—a stealth candidate if I ever saw one."

"What's a stealth candidate?" Jamie asked.

"Someone who runs for office without being specific about what they stand for. Well, lots of politicians do that. But a stealth candidate does it more thoroughly than most, and has a real hidden agenda. Many stealth candidates are supported by national organizations, too, and don't admit it. Anyway, Lisa Buel has certainly left the way wide open to surprise us all with anything she wants to do . . ."

"Hang on there, Maggie." Jamie's father got up and snatched the kettle, which was whistling, off the stove. "Maybe it *is* time for a reassessment. Can't hurt, can it?"

"Yes." Mrs. Crawford watched as her husband spooned co-coa powder into four mugs and poured water into them. "Yes, Dick, I'm afraid it can."

"Well, maybe she won't get in. Maybe Anna Pembar will beat her hollow. Ronnie! Cocoa's ready!"

Although Tessa's photos, which she'd developed at home after the meeting, were all good, it wasn't hard to decide which to run: the better of the two that showed both candi-dates and the moderator onstage. "I wish we could use the single shots, too," Jamie said before school Friday morning in the newspaper office. "But there's no more space on that page."

Matt looked up from checking the mechanical for the page in question. "You'll have to get used to that, Tessa. 'There's no space' is something every editor says about a hundred times an issue."

"No problem." Tessa smiled at Jamie. "Besides, that's got to be better than too much space."

"Yeah," Terry called from where he and Cindy were reorga-nizing some of the paper's files. "Important maxim, courtesy of Terry Gage: Empty papers don't sell."

Nomi rolled her eyes. "Let's go, Terry." She picked up Tessa's photo and fastened it to a piece of paper on which she'd already written size directions. "Time to get the baby to bed." She began gathering up her books.

Tessa looked inquiringly at Jamie.

"Take the last of the paper to the print shop," Jamie trans-lated.

Matt stood up, stretching. "And that's it for Volume 8, Number 1. It's a good first issue for the year, I think."

"The letters page is pretty thin," Jamie remarked. " 'Welcome Back,' 'Let's Go Wilson Wolves,' 'How I Plan to Study This Year.' "

"Blagh," Cindy commented, making a face on her way out. "If I'd known, I'd have gotten one of Jack's friends to write one. See you!"

"Next issue," Matt called after her, then turned to Jamie. "There'll be plenty of reaction next time to your editorial anyway. Especially since"—he glanced at Nomi—"we don't have an op-ed to balance it."

"Look, I'm sorry," Nomi said testily. "But like I told you, I'm an artist, not a writer. It wouldn't have been any good."

"She did consider doing it, Matt," Jamie told him.

"Okay, okay." Matt turned, picking up papers from his desk, and Jamie was surprised to see that he looked worried. Before she could say anything, though, Terry gave Nomi a little push. "We're outta here," he said. "You remember we're going to the movies tonight, Jamie?"

"Yes, sure," Jamie said absently, still watching Matt.

"Great. Come on, Nom'. If we don't get this to the shop in a hurry, we'll be late for homeroom. And they'll kill us for holding up the rest of the issue."

"Matt," Jamie asked quietly when Nomi and Terry had left and Tessa was putting on her cape, "do you think there's going to be real trouble about the editorial? Giving out condoms has been officially okayed, hasn't it? Even though it's controversial."

"Yes, it's been okayed. I don't think there'll be trouble. I admit I'd feel a lot better if we did have an op-ed, though." Matt patted her shoulder. "Who knows, Jamie? We'll just have to wait and see."

"I did try to acknowledge the other side in what I wrote."

"Yes, I know you did. And what you wrote is fine. You're not supposed to be balanced in an editorial, for Pete's sake. You were fair and accurate, not to mention persuasive, and that's all anyone can ask for." He gave Jamie's shoulder another pat. "Don't worry. It'll be okay. Now let's get out of here, you two. We'll be seeing enough of this place anyway in the next few months!"

"Date?" Tessa asked Jamie when they were outside; as it turned out, there was still a while before the first bell.

"Huh?"

"You and Terry? When he asked you to remember the movies? It sounded like you have a date with him."

Jamie laughed self-consciously. "It's not really a date," she said, "although we *are* going to the movies. Terry and Ernie Rivers and me."

Tessa smiled, a slow warm smile, but her eyes still held questions. "Three's a crowd, my mother says. So did my boyfriend last spring when I asked someone else to go out with us."

"It's not a crowd when the three are good friends," Jamie managed to say. But Tessa's words "my boyfriend" had stabbed through her like daggers. Jamie tried to freeze her face, to command it to show nothing.

"What're you seeing? What movie?"

Conversation, Jamie told herself. Casual conversation is called for. "You know, I have no idea." She stepped aside as Brandon Tomkins and Vicky Chase came out of the building, followed by Sam Mills and Karen Hodges, who continued past them into the parking lot.

"Hey, butch," Brandon said, stopping. "Got a new girl-friend?"

Tessa looked puzzled, then angry, but Vicky gave Brandon a sharp shove. "Don't mind him," she said to Tessa, smiling at her and at Jamie. "I hear you're photo editor," Vicky added, ignoring Brandon, who was looking Tessa up and down—leering, Jamie thought. "Congratulations. I love your cape."

"Hey, Tessa," Brandon said, reaching out as if to pull her aside—but Tessa moved away. "I figure I should warn . . ."

"Thanks," Tessa said calmly to Vicky, cutting Brandon off with a withering glance. "It's from a thrift shop."

"Cool," Vicky replied. "They've got the best stuff. I wish we had one in Wilson. There's a pretty good one in George-port, probably not as good as the ones you were used to in Boston, but I'll let you know next time I go, if you want to come."

"Thanks," Tessa said again. "Who," she asked Jamie when they'd left, "are those two? Ms. Gorgeous Sexy U.S.A. and Mr. Number One Macho Skinhead Creep?"

Jamie laughed. "That about sums it up," she said. "But Vicky's really nice as well as gorgeous and sexy. Brandon—well, he was the class bully when we were kids, along with his friend Al Checkers."

"Looks like he's still the class bully," Tessa observed. "What's with the girlfriend taunt?" When Jamie hesitated, she said, "Hey, we've got homophobic jerks in Boston, too. Anyone they don't like, they say stuff like that to."

"Yeah, Brandon's been saying stuff like that for years," Jamie answered carefully, willing herself not to blush and trying to ignore her suddenly sweating hands. "I guess I've kind of gotten used to it."

Tessa hesitated a moment, too, and Jamie felt she was trying to look right through her. But then Tessa put her camera bag down on the school steps and shifted her stack of books. "I love movies," she commented, as if nothing had happened, although her eyes followed Vicky and Brandon as they joined Sam and Karen in the parking lot. "But sometimes I watch the photography so much I don't pay attention to the plot. Which means I'm no good talking to other people afterward, unless they're photographers, too. Trouble is, I've never really met another photographer."

"Is that what you want to do?" Jamie asked, not daring to ask about the boyfriend Tessa had mentioned, not sure she wanted to know more about him anyway. "I mean professionally? Be a photographer?"

"Oh yes," Tessa answered emphatically. "A thousand times yes. It's the *only* thing I want to do professionally. People don't *see*, you know? I mean most people. They walk through the world, and their eyes—fall on things, but they don't really see what their eyes look at. They don't see the—oh, I don't know. The pain on other people's faces, or the joy, or the loneliness. They don't see the feelings of animals, or the way a tree stands out against the sky, or, I don't know, the alphabet in architecture, or the . . ."

"Whoa! The alphabet in architecture?"

"Yeah." Tessa pointed to the school's front door. "Look there. The hinges? They're L's. And that window at the top? That's an O."

"You're right." Jamie was intrigued now. "I bet you could find a neat alphabet down in the yacht basin. All those masts and lines. Or in the harbor."

"I already did. I like the working harbor better."

There was a pause, during which a seagull flew overhead, mewing raucously.

"A W!" Jamie cried, suddenly seeing one as the gull wheeled sharply. "A flying W!"

"Right!" Tessa faced Jamie. "How about you?" she asked. "What do you want to do?"

"Professionally, you mean?"

Tessa nodded.

"Something with newspapers," Jamie said, suddenly feeling a little shy, but wanting very much to tell her. "Sometimes I think I want to be a reporter, maybe even a foreign correspondent. Sometimes I think I want to be a columnist, or maybe an editor. But—well, you know how you want to make people see? I guess I want the same thing, really, only my medium is words instead of pictures. I want to give people accurate information so they can make intelligent decisions, and I also want to make them see, I don't know, the truth of things, I guess."

"We'd make a good team, then."

"Yeah." Jamie felt an odd rush of adrenaline. "Hey," she added recklessly, "maybe we should *be* a team this year, do stories together for the *Telegraph*. You know, at least sometimes. Maybe we could do a monthly photo feature."

"Sure. Why not? And maybe someday we'll both apply for jobs at the same paper and run into each other and have a big reunion."

"Or maybe we'll go to the same college."

"Maybe." Tessa pulled her cape closer around her. "But maybe I won't go at all. My big brother Phil's in college now, and he wants to go to medical school, too. My little sister Angela's really smart, and she should go. That's a lot of tuition money. Besides, you don't really need college for photography."

"Yeah, but if you want to go . . ."

Tessa smiled faintly. "I do. So I've applied to a bunch of places anyway, and I hope I get a scholarship. I do want to get away from—whoops!"

"What?"

"I'm sorry. I was going to say I want to get away from here. But that's not—well, it's your town."

Jamie laughed. "There's not a single kid here who doesn't want to get out of Wilson." She tried to read Tessa's face. "Do you miss Boston?" she asked.

"Yes," Tessa said, sounding almost grateful. "Yes, I do. Thanks for asking. I miss my friends and city noises and bustle—and even the homeless beggars. I put quarters in my pocket still, forgetting there's no one here to give them to. I miss buses and stores and museums and sirens and libraries and the subway and—yes, I miss Boston."

"But you'd like to go to church outdoors," Jamie said, "in the woods or on the beach with the gulls and the sandpipers."

Tessa laughed. "Yeah, well, I miss the Boston Public Garden, too, and Boston Common. I"—she leaned toward Jamie and dropped her voice—"am a mass of contradictions. I guess I'm many people. My best friend, Judy Evans, back in Boston used to say I don't know who I am, and that's why the cape and these." She indicated her rings and earrings and the star in her nose. "But she's wrong. Well, not all wrong. I know a lot of who I am, I think."

"Yes," said Jamie softly. "You seem to."

Tessa stretched, her long body making a slender arc as she bent back. "Good," she said, sounding satisfied. "Good.

That's how I'd like to seem." She snapped her body upright again. "So, is Terry your boyfriend?" she asked abruptly.

"No," Jamie answered, on guard herself now. "I mean—no. Um—what about your boyfriend? You mentioned him," she added hastily, embarrassed.

Tessa shrugged and her gaze shifted to the parking lot, where Jamie now saw Nomi and Clark getting out of Clark's car; Clark was holding the door for Nomi. "Kevin Allen Nottor's in Boston and Tessa Gillespie's in Wilson. And Kevin Allen's always been too sure of himself to be interesting. He's history, I think. Boys—men—are fine. Lots of them are downright nice, and some are ver-r-ry sexy. But right now I'm too busy, I think. And I haven't seen much here that interests me." She glanced at Jamie as if checking for her reaction. "Yes. Too busy. Too preoccupied. You, too?"

"I—well, sure. Right," Jamie sputtered even as her mind flashed *LIAR* to her in bold-face capital italics. "I never thought of it in quite that way. But, yeah. I agree."

Tessa's eyes met Jamie's. "Sorry. That's probably none of my business. Judy also used to tell me I'm too intense. Too nosy, too, sometimes."

"No, no, it's not that. It's just—you're pretty direct, you know?"

"What's the point in not being direct? I hate playing mind games, word games, any games like that with people. It's a waste of time. Tomorrow I could get hit by a truck or diagnosed with cancer. I want to make every minute of my life count."

Jamie took a deep breath. "Me, too," she said lamely.

"I sound sure of myself," Tessa was saying, "and most of the time I am, about most things. Not everything, though." She put her head on one side and smiled faintly. "Are we going to be friends?" she asked softly.

"I—I'd like that."

"So would I." Tessa picked up her camera bag and her books. "I didn't want to move here, and when we did, and I first walked into Wilson High and saw all those strangers' faces, I told myself to keep to myself, that I probably wouldn't find any true friends. I guess I was kind of snobby. Fishermen, I thought; fishermen and car mechanics." She laughed. "Not that my family's any better, but snobby Tessa decided it would be okay to be a loner because then she could concentrate on studying and photography. I guess I might have been wrong about some of that, hm?"

Jamie smiled. "I guess you might have been."

"Well, friend," said Tessa, "I've got to go. But I'm glad we had this talk. We'll have another sometime, okay?"

"Of course okay. I'm glad you came to Wilson," Jamie added awkwardly. "And I'm glad you'll be on the paper, and . . ."

"Hey, let's leave it at that," Tessa answered. "Otherwise I'll get stuck-up!"

It was freezing cold in the movie theater, as if the management had forgotten to turn off the air conditioning now that it was fall. At first Terry sat in the middle, between Jamie and Ernie, but after about fifteen minutes, Terry whispered to Jamie, "Let's switch; being cold makes me want to cuddle with Ernie. We'd both better cuddle with you instead."

They changed places, ignoring the grumbles of "Sit down!" from behind. Ernie seemed tense and preoccupied, even when all three of them huddled together as best they could. Jamie, in the middle, actually began to feel warm, but then Terry whispered, "It's like being by a fire, you know? One side's warm and the other's freezing. Let's get out of here."

Jamie agreed readily, for the movie wasn't all that good, and Ernie, especially, didn't seem to be enjoying it.

"Hungry?" asked Terry, once they were outside, and warmer.

"Sure," said Jamie.

"Ernie?"

Ernie shrugged.

"Look," Jamie said, "we could go on back to Wilson and then you guys could, I don't know—be together without me tagging along. I feel sort of in the way."

"You're not in the way," Ernie said quickly, emphatically, as if forcing himself to emerge from his bad mood. "Really. Come on, let's go get something to eat. That was a good idea."

So they sat over fries and enormous hamburgers and Cokes in a loud mall restaurant where they had to shout to be heard. As it was, Terry and Jamie did most of the talking.

"I'm so full," Terry announced, pushing his plate away when it was empty, "that I'm going to have to roll out of here."

Ernie laughed, too loudly, Jamie thought, sure he was forcing it, and when they got to the front and had paid, Terry, as if desperate to make Ernie laugh genuinely, surprised Jamie by suddenly getting down on the floor and somersaulting out the door, which Jamie quickly opened for him and held. Several people stared, and one or two laughed. A middle-aged man, who had to step aside to let Terry's curled body roll out the door, muttered "Kids!" disgustedly.

"No, no," Terry said, scrambling to his feet, "it's 'Kids *today*.' You've got to remember the 'today' part, because," he shouted as Jamie, laughing in spite of herself, although Ernie looked painfully embarrassed, pulled him away—"because kids today are a lot worse than kids were yesterday, when you were a kid, or maybe day before yesterday, when . . ."

"Drunk," the man muttered as he darted angrily inside.

Terry brushed himself off and draped his arm over Ernie's shoulders. "Why do adults always think people our age are drunk when we're just—I don't know. Exuberant?"

Ernie pushed Terry away. "Don't, Terry," he said softly.

Terry froze, his face stricken. "Sorry," he said stiffly.

"I—me, too," Ernie said. "Sorry, I mean. I—I'm just no good tonight, I guess. My dad—oh hell, never mind."

"What?" asked Terry. "Your dad what?"

But Ernie just shook his head.

Jamie glanced at Terry, who shrugged. "How about we drive around for a bit?" she suggested. "Or go home to Wilson and to Sloan's Beach, maybe, and walk?" She touched Ernie's arm shyly. "Would that help any?"

Ernie gave a short, bitter laugh. "Going home sure wouldn't," he said. "I mean going home to my house. Going home's the problem." He smiled thinly. "Sure. Let's drive to Sloan's Beach. Anywhere's okay; Sloan's Beach is fine."

He headed for the parking lot, and Jamie and Terry quickly fell into step behind him.

"What a dumb movie," Jamie said, trying to fill the awkward pause as they got into Terry's car; Ernie got into the back, maneuvering around Jamie to do so, even though she tried to step aside to let him get in front with Terry. "We could write a better one easily."

"Yeah," Terry agreed, too heartily, as he backed the car out of its space. "Let's see . . . Okay, I've got it. There's this lonely typewriter . . ."

"Who falls in love with a computer," Jamie supplied.

"Only the computer's really in love with a copier . . ."

"But the copier likes the fax machine instead . . ."

Jamie glanced in the rearview mirror at Ernie, who was staring outside, not participating, probably not even listening, she thought—and she and Terry, after a few more feeble attempts at silliness, lapsed into silence.

The moon hung brightly over the water at Sloan's Beach, but they needed the flashlight from Terry's glove compartment to avoid slipping on rockweed. For a while they walked in silence, and Jamie, sandwiched uneasily between Terry and Ernie, hoped that the steady cold wind and the even sound of the sea lapping against the shore would calm whatever demons were in Ernie's mind.

Finally Terry stopped. "My thinking place," he said lightly to Ernie, indicating a large flat rock on which he and Jamie often sat. "Have a seat. Or would you rather go on walking?"

"Walking, I guess."

"Okay." Terry threw back his shoulders and took a deep breath. "Walking's good. Clears the cobwebs, right, Jamie?"

"Something like that," Jamie said quietly, watching Ernie.

"So what did your dad do?" Terry asked, watching him also. "Come on, Ernie, maybe you'll feel better if you tell us. Jamie won't mind. Will you, Jamie?"

"No, but maybe Ernie will. I could leave. I can walk home from here . . ."

"I don't mind," Ernie said. He drew a deep breath. "Okay. I

told my father I had a date tonight. You know, implying it was with a girl. He's been bugging me about seeing Terry so much," Ernie explained to Jamie. "So he gives me this big wink and slaps me on the back and says, 'Great, son, great. Don't do anything I wouldn't do.' That's the first time he's called me son since I stopped playing Little League."

"Bastard," Terry said softly; Jamie saw him reach for Ernie's hand.

But Ernie moved away. "It's other stuff, too. Yesterday at practice? A couple of the guys were talking about some kid at swimming camp this summer. They called him a faggot and said they used to duck him and hold him under a lot. One day they all left the locker room when he came in, and then they told the coach that he'd been, you know, eyeing them. And so the camp administration threw him out. Reminded me of my dad; he was an army recruiter for a while, and he's bragged a million times that he could tell a guy was gay just by the way he walked. He ought to hire himself out to our pastor; last Sunday in church, you know, Lord's Assembly"—Ernie's voice was shaking now—"the pastor said the sex ed part of the new health curriculum's going to cause a lot of trouble. He said he'd do everything he could to keep fornicators and homosexuals and pederasts out of Wilson. And a lot of people in the congregation kind of murmured 'Yes.' My dear parents included."

He turned to Jamie. "Your friend Nomi? She was right there a couple of pews away with her folks, and they were smiling and nodding along with everyone else. Good old Al Checkers was there, too. He and his family looked like they wanted to jump up and cheer, you know, kill the faggots or something. I could almost hear him saying it."

Ernie looked at Terry, as if pleading with him, and once more Jamie felt like an intruder. She tried to move away inconspicuously when Ernie spoke again, his voice low. "Terry, I . . ." He turned away, fists clenched.

Terry stepped toward him, standing close without touching. "It's okay, Ernie," Jamie heard him say, his voice catching a little as he spoke. "I've told you we can be friends for now. It's okay. Let's do that. I'd rather be just friends with you than lose you."

But as she quickly walked away, Jamie saw the tears on Terry's face.

FIVE

Editorial
THE BOTTOM LINE

Starting in October, condoms will be available to all students in the nurse's office (see announcement, page 5). There's been a lot of controversy about that. Some people say that distributing condoms encourages people to have sex and makes them irresponsible, because it makes them think nothing bad can happen to them as a result. Maybe that would be true if we didn't have a new sex ed curriculum at the same time. But all health classes, from freshmen on up through seniors, have already learned that condoms aren't foolproof, that they have to be used the right way, and that even if they are, they can break. Using a condom doesn't result in completely safe sex. It just results in saf*er* sex.

But some people say high school kids shouldn't have sex at all, unsafe, safe, or safer. They say we aren't ready; we aren't mature enough; we're too careless. That's probably true of some people. And I hope those people know who they are. But what I don't see is how a school administration or faculty can think they can completely prevent kids from having sex. Even if you know that it's not a good idea, that doesn't mean you're always strong enough to resist. There are lots of pressures on people to have sex, and sometimes they're hard to ignore. At least if kids use condoms, they're protected during those times when they can't say no.

It's true that abstinence is the only way to guarantee that you won't get pregnant or get a sexually transmitted disease. We've all learned that in health class. But it's not true that everyone is going to practice abstinence just because adults say that's the thing to do. Lots of adults don't practice abstinence, so how can they expect kids to? Isn't it better to be safe than sorry, as the saying goes?

The bottom line is that not using a condom can mean a girl's life—and perhaps a boy's, too—may have to be put on hold or may even be ruined because of an unplanned pregnancy. It can also mean that a girl's life or a boy's life could get messed up for a while because of a curable sexually transmitted disease. And it could mean that a girl's or a boy's life gets cut off—ended—because of AIDS. The bottom line here is that condoms save lives. Shouldn't the school do everything it can to help save lives, too?

—Jamie Crawford, Editor in Chief

The Telegraph *invites Op-Ed replies to this editorial and all others, especially replies that dissent from the views expressed here.*

"Jamie, it's good," Mrs. Crawford said Sunday night when Jamie showed the editorial to her parents right after dinner, deciding it would be a good idea to give them a preview before the paper came out the next morning. "Really good, but . . ."

"But what? What, Mom?"

Jamie's mother looked at her husband over the rim of her coffee mug, then put the mug down. "But I think you'd better be prepared for some fireworks."

"I don't see what the big deal is," Ronnie put in, grinning. "Big deal over a little piece of rubber! That's all Fred's brother says it is. Can I go out, Mom?"

"Where?"

"Just next door to Fred's."

"How about homework?" asked Mr. Crawford.

"Just math."

"How much?"

"Five word problems."

Mrs. Crawford raised her eyebrows. "Homework first," she told him. "Then maybe you can *call* Fred."

"The quicker, the sooner, Ron," said Mr. Crawford, winking. "Skedaddle. That little piece of rubber, as Ronnie so indelicately put it," he went on when Ronnie had left, grumbling, "is, I think, going to become a hot issue if Lisa Buel gets elected to the school committee. Is there any more coffee?"

When Jamie got to school Monday morning, she saw that the *Telegraph*'s bin by the main entrance was already half empty. With some trepidation, she made her way to her homeroom, trying to look nonchalant. But a chorus of approval greeted her.

"Cool editorial, Jamie!"

"Yeah, Jamie, way to go!"

"All right!"

"Geeze," said Jamie, walking more confidently to her desk and seeing that virtually every paper in the room was open to the editorial page, "isn't anyone reading anything else?"

"You know how it is," said Terry. "Anything with sex really gets people's attention. Congratulations, Jamie; everyone loves it."

"Not quite everyone." Jamie saw that Nomi was sitting quietly in her seat at the back, reading her social studies book—or, Jamie was sure, pretending to read it. "Excuse me."

She walked over to Nomi and slipped into the empty seat beside her. "Hi," she said.

Nomi looked up briefly, then dropped her eyes back to her book, murmuring "Hi."

"Did you read it?"

"Did I read what?"

"The editorial, pea brain!"

"Yes, I read it."

"Well? What do you think? I tried to give the other side."

"Oh, come on, Jamie." Nomi closed her book. "You gave the other side only to shoot it down. You know, I don't understand you anymore. You say you're for life and you talk like you're worried about people's futures. But you're just worried about their bodies, physical things. I don't know about you, but there's more to me than a body."

"Of course there is. To everyone. Come on, Nomi, read the editorial again. I'm saying that kids who get pregnant or sick can mess up a lot more than their bodies."

"You just don't get it, do you? I'm surprised at you. But you really don't get it."

Jamie thrust her hands out in frustration. "I do get it, I think. I agree that abstinence is the best way. But you're assuming that people are a lot stronger than they are. You're being idealistic, and that's great, but . . ."

"And you're being hypocritical. If you assume people are going to be weak, they're going to be weak. If you assume they can be strong, they'll at least try."

"And if they fail?" Out of the corner of her eye, Jamie saw that several other kids had come closer and were now clustered around them. "Look, let's say a kid's trying very hard not to sleep with her boyfriend. She wants to wait till she's married, and she's a good person. But she and her boyfriend really love each other, and one night they're watching TV or something and there's no one home, and they're making out a little . . ."

Someone—Brandon Tomkins—said, "Oh, wow," sarcastically, and a girl in the back squeaked, "No, John, no, I'm saving myself for my husband."

Jamie glared at them and continued. "And they both get excited."

"And then they should stop making out," Nomi said quickly, stepping on the sarcastic tongue clickings and mock-horrified indrawn breaths that followed Jamie's remark. "They should remind themselves that if they really love each other, they want to protect each other, so . . ."

"So they use a condom," Brandon said, echoed by several others—but not, Jamie noticed with surprise, by his friend Al Checkers, who looked uncharacteristically uncomfortable.

"But, butchie," Brandon called to Jamie, "what does a dyke want with a condom anyway?"

"Stuff it, Brandon," Vicky said.

"Anytime, baby, anytime," Brandon replied promptly, leering.

There was a chorus of rough laughter.

Nomi opened her social studies book again. "You're all hopeless."

"Nomi," Jamie began, "look, let's . . ."

But by then Nomi had turned away, back to her book.

After homeroom, Terry came over to Jamie. "Some people can't be convinced of some things, no matter how eloquent your prose. Going to English?"

"Yeah," Jamie muttered around the lump in her throat, rummaging in her desk for her books. "Yeah, okay."

Nomi stayed away from Jamie the rest of that day, sitting with Clark at lunch instead of with the newspaper editors, where she usually sat. Tessa, though, paused at the door to the cafeteria, near where that day's teacher-monitor was deep in conversation with another teacher, and then wove her way through the crowds of noisy students to the newspaper table.

"That editorial was really good, Jamie," she said, balancing her tray.

"Thanks." Jamie moved her chair over. "Have a seat. You know just about everyone, I think."

Cindy smiled. "I like your school committee photo, Tessa. Nice job." She doffed her baseball cap, and Jack, who usually ate at that table even though the other reporters didn't, said, "Yeah, great photo."

"Thanks. But it wasn't much. Just a three-person mug shot. That's nothing compared to Jamie's editorial."

Jack nodded. "We were just talking about that."

"The teachers were talking about it, too," Terry said, arriving, his tray heaped with food. "I went past the teachers' room on the way here and it sounded to me like someone was chewing Matt out about it. I heard bad words like 'unbalanced' and 'biased.' "

Cindy groaned. "What else is an editorial supposed to be, for Pete's sake? People are so dumb! It's like they've got it backwards. They want editorials to be balanced and news stories to be biased."

"Or they think news stories are biased whenever they report on stuff they don't like," said Jamie, "even when the stories are objective. Look, Matt says that if a newspaper doesn't stir people up, it's dead. So we're alive, is all. That's pretty good for the first issue of the year."

"Only a scant hundred left to go," said Terry.

Jack grinned. "Whoa! Can we keep it up?"

"Is that really true?" Tessa asked. "A hundred left to go?"

"Figure of speech," said Terry. "Hyperbole, actually. It's more like, I don't know, sixteen." Then he lowered his voice. "Possible enemy approaching."

Jamie looked in the direction Terry had nodded and saw Clark Alman heading for their table. "Could be," she said, but secretly she hoped he was coming with a conciliatory message from Nomi.

He did seem friendly enough. "Interesting editorial, Jamie," he said. "I don't agree with it, as you can imagine. I thought it was well written, though."

Tessa patted Jamie's hand. Terry winked; it was a joke between him and Jamie that when people didn't like the content of something but felt they should say something good about it, they said it was well written.

"And," Clark went on, "it's an important subject. We've been kicking it around in our youth group—you know, at

Lord's Assembly—and we'd like to have a sort of debate about it." He smiled. "Only we've been having trouble finding anyone from the pro-condom side. We don't want someone like Brandon with hormones instead of brains. So I was wondering, would you come to one of our meetings and represent your point of view? That condoms are good?"

"That condoms save lives," Jamie countered evenly. She hesitated, struck by the irony of Clark's asking her to air her opinion at his church when he wouldn't air his in the paper. But at least if she agreed, there'd *be* a debate about it. "Sure," she said finally. "When?"

"Some Sunday night in October," Clark replied. "Seven o'clock, at the church. We meet in the basement. I'll let you know the exact date. Hey, thanks."

"You're welcome," Jamie called after him.

"Geeze," said Tessa, echoing Jamie's thought, "if he's so anxious to have a discussion, how come he wouldn't do it in the paper?"

"Yeah," Cindy said. "Didn't he write a couple of op-eds last year?"

"Yes," said Terry. "He did."

Jamie picked up her sandwich. "Well, maybe he doesn't like writing anymore. I guess we should be glad that at least he's willing to talk. He's really okay—I think."

The next day was the school committee election, so Jamie stopped Nomi in the hall at dismissal. "Tell your mom good luck from me."

"Thanks." But Nomi turned away without smiling and walked on toward her locker.

"Nomi!" Jamie ran after her. "Can't we disagree and still be friends?"

"I don't know. I honestly don't know. It's too important an issue, Jamie. Not agreeing means we're very wide apart, morally, sort of. I mean, it'd be like not agreeing on abortion, or homosexuality, or murder, or something like that."

Jamie felt a sudden chill. "Well, we probably don't agree on most of those. But can't we agree to disagree? Look, you probably know this—Clark's invited me to debate at your youth group. It seems to me that's a healthy way to deal with disagreements. Maybe we can all learn from each other."

"Maybe. We can learn what the other side thinks, anyway. But I don't see how you and I can be friends if we're so far apart. It's hard for me to go on being friends with someone who I think believes in immorality."

Jamie hesitated. Then, trying not to sound angry, she said, "Did it ever occur to you that I might think what you believe is just as immoral? But that doesn't mean I can't like you as a person, respect you, want to be your friend."

"That's nice," Nomi said coldly, twirling her combination. "But I'm not sure I can do the same."

Jamie's eyes filled with sudden tears. "I don't believe this is happening." She put her hand on Nomi's arm. "Come on, Nom', we've been friends since we were little kids. We've grown up together; we've . . ."

"We're not little kids anymore. And I guess we've grown in different ways."

"I . . ." But Jamie's voice caught in her throat, and she realized it would probably be futile to protest further. "Okay," she said. "But please tell your mom good luck from me. I hope you can still manage to do that."

"Yeah," Nomi said with a ghost of a smile. "Yeah, I can. Jamie," she added, as Jamie turned to leave, "Jamie, I . . . I'm sorry."

. . .

Much later that night, when Jamie was upstairs doing homework, the phone rang. Hoping it was Nomi, she ran to the extension in the hall, but before she got to it, she heard her mother's voice from downstairs saying, "Thank you, Morris. I really appreciate it. I guess you've got your work cut out for you now . . . Yes, of course I'll still come to meetings when I can. I hope Anna will also . . . Yes, we thought so, too. I'll tell her . . . Thanks, Morris. Goodbye."

Jamie heard her mother hang up and then come to the foot of the stairs. "Jamie?" she called.

"Yes? I'm right here." Jamie went halfway down.

"That was Morris Just—head of the school committee? He said to congratulate you on your editorial. He said it was a brave thing to write."

"That was nice of him." Jamie hesitated. "Did Mrs. Pembar lose the election? What you said kind of sounded like it."

"I'm afraid so," her mother answered. "Lisa Buel got in by about twenty votes."

October

SIX

"Oh, good grief!" Mr. Crawford thumped the town's weekly newspaper, the Wilson *News-Courier*, angrily down next to his plate of bacon and eggs.

"What?" asked his wife, pouring coffee. "Jamie, Ronnie, more toast?"

"No thanks, Mom," Jamie said absently. It was Saturday, the day before the debate at Lord's Assembly, and she was already feeling nervous. But she was meeting Tessa that morning and hoped that would distract her temporarily; she didn't want to think anymore about the debate till that night.

"Uh-uh." Ronnie gulped down the remainder of his milk, jammed his baseball cap on his head, and headed for the door.

"How about 'No thank you, Mom'?" Mr. Crawford said, his eyes on the paper again.

"Yeah, whatever."

Mr. Crawford looked up. "Ronnie!" he said sharply.

Ronnie paused, his hand on the doorknob. "Sorry." He rolled his eyes. "No thank you, Mom."

"That's better," said Mr. Crawford.

Mrs. Crawford put Ronnie's dishes in the sink. "Lunch at twelve-thirty, Ronnie."

"I don't think I'll be here," Jamie put in, scraping up the last of her eggs.

"Oh?" her mother said mildly as Ronnie escaped. "Where will you be?"

"With Tessa. We're going to work on a sort of photo essay we want to do for the paper. We'll probably get a burger or something, okay?"

Her mother smiled. "Sure. Dinner's at six," Mrs. Crawford called as Jamie put on her jacket. "I'll excuse you from the breakfast dishes, Jamie, but not the supper ones. And did you or Ronnie get the trash ready for the dump this morning? You both forgot last night."

"Yes," Jamie said sheepishly. "I did it. Sorry about forgetting." She opened the back door.

"Jamie, wait," said her father. "I think you ought to see this bit in the paper before you go out." He handed her the Wilson *News-Courier*, open to the "School News" page:

SCHOOL TO DISTRIBUTE CONDOMS
Controversy Erupts

From this month on, Wilson High School will make condoms available in the nurse's office every Friday afternoon to any student who wants them, Principal Ralph Bartholomew announced at a school committee meeting on Wednesday. In September, the distribution was the subject of an editorial in the school's newspaper, the Wilson High *Telegraph*, and subsequent letters to the editor in that paper showed widespread support for the distribution among the students. A small group, however, led by Clark Alman, president of the youth group at Lord's Assembly Church, when interviewed by this reporter, expressed disapproval of the idea. "It's sending the wrong message," Alman said. "It's telling kids it's okay to go out and have sex, saying that nothing bad will happen if they do. But that's not the point. The point is that it's not just dangerous to have sex if you're not married. It's immoral, too."

Alman's sentiments were echoed by Lisa Buel, recently elected to the Wilson School Committee to fill the vacancy left by Barbara Cochran, who moved away unexpectedly last summer. "The only way to prevent dangerous diseases like syphilis and AIDS," Buel said, "is not to have sex at all. Condoms break, after all. But young Clark is right. That's not really the point. The point is that sex before marriage is immoral. The moral fabric of our country is growing weaker every day, what with homosexuality, drug abuse, alcohol abuse, unwed mothers, and fathers who don't support their kids. It's time we took a long, hard look in every community at what we're teaching our children and what values we're showing them."

Buel, who said she is not a member of any national fundamentalist organization, told the *News-Courier* that she is in the process of organizing a group called Families for Traditional Values here in Wilson. "Anyone interested can call me at 222–9673," she said.

In her editorial, Jamie Crawford, editor in chief of the Wilson High *Telegraph*, said that condoms save lives. "Lots of adults don't practice abstinence," she wrote, "so how can they expect kids to? Isn't it better to be safe than sorry, as the saying goes?"

Jamie handed the paper back to her father. Before she could comment, he said, "Jamie, I don't mean to interfere, but I really do think that this could get to be a very big issue. It would probably be a good idea for you and the paper to stay out of it as much as possible."

"Oh, no, it wouldn't," Jamie said hotly, Lisa Buel's reference to homosexuality still burning before her eyes. "I'm not going to let the *Telegraph* run away from any issue, Dad. Papers can't ignore controversy."

"I just don't want you to get hurt, honey. I know you're a good editor, but . . ."

Jamie kissed the top of his head. "But I wouldn't be if I ran away scared. Back by dinnertime, Mom."

As she left, she heard her mother say, "Lisa Buel didn't mention starting a group about traditional values when she put her name up for that vacancy. And not being a member of 'any national fundamentalist organization' doesn't mean she's not getting support from one. I told you she was a stealth candidate with a secret agenda."

"You did," Jamie heard her father answer. "It's going to be an interesting year, at least till the regular election in March, and maybe after it as well. I just hope Jamie's not going to find herself right smack in the middle of it."

Tessa was waiting in front of the town hall, her camera bag slung over her shoulder; Jamie studied her for a moment from across the street. Tessa was looking toward the town square, shading her eyes with her hand, apparently watching two little boys ride their tricycles around the granite honor roll, on which were engraved names of servicemen and women from Wilson who'd died in various wars. Even at a distance, Tessa's beauty brought a catch to Jamie's throat. But it's not just that, Jamie thought. It's lots of things, intangible ones . . .

Which I'd better stop thinking about, Jamie told herself, crossing the street.

Tessa turned as Jamie approached. "Hi. Did you see the town paper?"

"My dad showed it to me. Hi."

"What gets me," said Tessa, "is that that Buel woman was talking about more than just condoms. 'Traditional values'—that's more. My father says sometimes what that really means is that someone wants little cookie-cutter people, all the same. I think he's right, don't you?" Without waiting for an answer, she touched Jamie's arm lightly. "Hey, let's go. Let's find some pictures."

They spent the morning prowling along the trail that ran through the marsh opposite the yacht basin; they had decided to do a nature essay, and Tessa wanted to photograph as many birds as possible before winter set in. "I'd like to come back in the winter, though, too," she said when she and Jamie decided to take a break.

"So would I." Jamie sat on a bench at the edge of the marsh and beckoned Tessa to join her. "The grass here is beautiful when there's been a frost." She looked carefully for the right words to make the marsh seem as special to Tessa as it did to her. "It's covered with woolly white threads on cold mornings, or with silver filigree if the sun's out. And the ice isn't flat and boring. It's got—it's etched with frozen swirls and bubbles, and sometimes water runs under it and catches the light where it's really shallow, and in that stream we crossed . . ."

"Etched," repeated Tessa softly. "It sounds perfect. You *are* a writer. I'd never have thought of that word."

"Maybe not," said Jamie. "But I'd never be able to show the ice well in a photograph."

"So we really are a team."

"Right. We are." Jamie reached her hand toward Tessa's, then pulled it back, unsure how Tessa would react. Tessa didn't seem to notice the gesture, and for a moment they both fell silent, watching a pair of geese fly overhead.

"Are you nervous about tomorrow night?" Tessa asked. "At Lord's Assembly?"

Jamie picked up a stick and began peeling off its bark. "A little," she admitted. "No, more than a little; I like writing better than talking. And I don't know what to expect, you know? I think I'm more nervous because Nomi's in the group than I am because of what I'm going to say or what the other side's going to say."

"How come?"

"Because Nomi's my friend." She hesitated. "She used to be my best friend. I guess Terry's that now, but Nomi and I were really close till a couple of years ago. But she was still my second-best friend." Jamie dropped the stick and its bark peelings. Tessa can't be interested in this, she thought.

But Tessa had turned toward her attentively, her eyes searching Jamie's face. "And?" she asked. "What happened a couple of years ago?"

"I guess Nomi and I started going in different directions," Jamie told her carefully. "And now we're even further apart, because she thinks we can't be friends if we don't agree. That makes me sad."

"It's crazy." Tessa stretched her arms in front of her, palms out and fingers locked. Jamie noticed her nail polish again, though she hadn't thought of it consciously in a while, and her rings, especially the star one. "People can be friends even if they're different from each other," Tessa said. Her eyes met Jamie's as she freed her fingers and moved her hands back. "Look at you and me. Look at you and Terry. I'm a city person; you're a country person. Terry's a boy; you're a girl."

"But you and I have things in common," Jamie managed to say. "At least it seems that way so far. And Terry and I"—she floundered evasively—"we do, too. Some pretty important ones." She stopped, worried that she might say too much.

Tessa looked out over the marsh. "Nomi has a steady boyfriend, right? But maybe you're too busy for Terry to be your boyfriend, or maybe you don't want a boyfriend . . ." She paused, as if waiting for Jamie to speak, and then continued. "And I'm too busy and too far away for Kevin Allen to be mine." She turned, smiling at Jamie. "Here's to independent womanhood, right?"

"Right," said Jamie, half hoping that Tessa had guessed about her, but not quite daring to ask or to say anything about it—not knowing how to say it, either. So she just raised her hand as if she were holding a glass. "Independent woman-hood."

They had lunch in the dark little sandwich shop in the center of town, nearly empty now that the tourist season was almost over; the retirees who came in the fall usually pre-ferred to eat in the fancy white clapboard inn that sat on the hill looking down on the center. After lunch, Jamie showed Tessa the town's small museum, open only on weekends now that it was fall, and took her through the restored eighteenth-century house that was part of its exhibit.

"Can I come hear your debate tomorrow?" Tessa asked when they stood outside the house in the late-afternoon sun.

"I guess you could come," Jamie said slowly. "I don't know. I'll be more nervous, though, if you're there."

"Then I won't. I don't want to make you nervous. But call me when it's over and tell me how it went, okay?"

"Okay."

"I'll be thinking of you, wishing you luck. Maybe I'll even cross my fingers."

Jamie laughed.

They stood there in the waning light, smiling at each other.

"It's been a wonderful day," Tessa said.

"Yes. It has."

There was another long silence. And then Tessa put her hands gently on Jamie's shoulders and drew Jamie close to her in a swift hug. "Thank you," she said, stepping back.

"No—no," Jamie said, flustered. "No, I should thank *you*, for agreeing to do photo essays."

"We're a team, remember?" Tessa's head was slightly cocked, and she regarded Jamie with a half-hesitant, half-amused look as she pulled her red cape tighter around her body. "I'd better go. Call me tomorrow night," she tossed over her shoulder as she left. "And good luck. Take a deep breath before you speak. My father had to make a speech once and he said that helped."

"Okay," Jamie called as Tessa disappeared into the rapidly falling darkness. "I will. Good night."

When Tessa was gone, Jamie stood quietly for a few minutes. She knew it was only her imagination, but she felt diminished, empty, now that Tessa was gone.

And still reeling from her hug.

"You're in love, that's why, you blithering idiot," Terry said when she called him that night, ostensibly to go over some of what she was going to say in the debate.

"I don't know. Maybe I'm just glad that I've found a friend. In any case, she's straight."

"You have friends," Terry pointed out. "You have me. You have Nomi . . ."

"I'm not so sure of Nomi."

"She'll come around. But we're not talking about friends, are we? Hmmm?"

"Don't be catty, Terry," Jamie said, annoyed. "I told you she's straight. How was the swim meet?"

"You're changing the subject."

"I know. How was it?"

There was a pause. "Okay," Terry said finally. "We won, anyway."

"You don't sound wildly enthusiastic. How was Ernie?"

"Beautiful. We won because of him."

"So how come you're not out celebrating with the team?"

"He is, I guess. Out with the team."

"But you're not? You always celebrate with our teams when they win. You interview the players, and—"

Terry cut her off. "Yeah, I know, but this is different." He paused.

"What's wrong?" Jamie asked when he didn't seem about to continue.

"Nothing. Well, okay. Something. I tried to hug him afterward, you know, like anyone would. I mean, everyone was hugging and slapping butt and stuff. But he turned away and he wouldn't let me touch him. Hell, I must've touched everyone else!"

There was a longer pause; Jamie was about to break it when Terry spoke again. "He's terrified, Jamie." Terry's voice was so soft Jamie could barely hear it. "Terrified of me. Of himself, too, and what he feels. And of his parents. Maybe more of them than of anything, of what they've taught him, what they believe. I know he loves me, but like he said, he can't, you know, act on it. He can't even face himself, let alone what he feels about me. And the awful thing is, I know he's in terrible pain."

"Oh, Terry," Jamie said lamely. "I'm sorry. Really, really sorry."

"I probably should stop seeing him, but instead I've been giving him books, you know, taking the good ones out of the library. Both libraries; I even found a couple at school."

"Yeah, a couple," said Jamie sarcastically, thinking of the list in her hidden box, her joy at finding a few of the books on it, and her frustration at not finding more.

"Right. But at least there are some. And I'm thinking of going to Georgeport to see if I can find others. But I don't think it's books he needs as much as someone to talk to."

"How about someone in Georgeport?" She remembered an article she'd cut out during the summer. "I think there's some kind of counseling thing for gay kids; I might have the number. I could . . ."

But Terry cut her off again. "He'd never go. He gave the books back to me so fast I'm sure he didn't read them."

Jamie hesitated. "Maybe he'd talk to me. I know he hasn't

yet, really, but like I said before, it might be easier for him to talk to someone who's still a Maybe."

"Are you?" Terry asked after a short, voiceless laugh. "Still a Maybe? I thought . . ."

"Terry, I don't know, okay? Maybe I am, maybe I'm not. I'm not as sure as you. What's more important for Ernie is that I'm not involved."

There was another pause. "Okay," Terry said at last. "I guess you might as well. Go ahead and try, anyway."

"First thing Monday," Jamie told him. "First chance I get."

SEVEN

The youth group meeting was held in the basement of Lord's Assembly Church, where there was a comfortable living room with a fireplace. Folding chairs had been arranged in a double-row semicircle facing the fireplace, and a table with three chairs behind it had been placed in front of the semicircle for Jamie, Clark, and the moderator. A longer table, holding napkins, pitchers, a coffee urn, two jugs of cider, and several plates of cookies and slices of cake, stretched across the back of the room.

When Jamie arrived, a few adults—Nomi's mother, Lisa Buel, the pastor of Lord's Assembly Church and his wife— were already seated in the back. The adults were in a straight row of chairs behind the semicircle, which the youth group members, Al Checkers among them, were gradually filling. Nomi came in soon after Jamie and Clark took their places; she went right up to the front table, hugged Clark, and whispered something to him. Then she turned to Jamie and gave her a quick, faint smile, without speaking. Before Jamie had time to react, Nomi had fled to the first row, where she sat in the middle, directly opposite Clark.

"Good evening, ladies and gentlemen," the moderator announced. "We are pleased tonight to have a guest from Wilson High, Jamie Crawford, editor in chief of the school newspaper, who will debate our own Clark Alman on the controversial condom issue. Here with us also are Mr. Bruce Donnelly, our beloved pastor, and his wife, Susan. Mrs. Lisa Buel of the school committee is here as well. I believe Mrs. Buel has something to say before we begin. Lisa?"

Lisa Buel walked to the front of the room. "Thank you. I don't want to hold things up, but I'd just like to say that I've put a sign-up sheet and some pamphlets on the refreshment table for anyone who's interested in finding out more about our new group, Families for Traditional Values, FTV for short. We'll be holding our charter meeting tomorrow night in this very room, and everyone is welcome. Tell your parents, kids," she said to the youth group members, "and come yourselves if you like. All our meetings will be open to everyone."

"Thank you, Lisa," said the moderator. "And now let's begin. Jamie and Clark will each make an opening statement, and they will each have the opportunity to rebut what the other has said. After that, I'll probably ask them a few questions myself, and then we'll open the meeting to questions and comments from the floor. At the end, Jamie and Clark can each make a closing statement, if they wish. Jamie, as our guest, would you go first, please?"

Jamie felt her stomach turn over, and was instantly aware of perspiration rolling down her sides. But she tried to ignore that. "Sure," she said in the firmest voice she could muster. "Thank you. Some of you," she began, glancing down at her notes, "may have read the editorial I wrote in this year's first issue of the Wilson High *Telegraph*. But it's been about a

month since then, so let me just go over some of the points I
made, in which I still believe . . ."

For an hour after the debate, Jamie sat at home in the
kitchen talking about it and drinking cocoa with her parents.
Then she spent another hour on the phone with Tessa. And at
last she went to her room and got ready for bed. But she
couldn't sleep, so she went to her closet, took the yellow notebook out of its box, propped herself up in bed, and started
writing:

> Well, it's over, anyway, that debate. I'm not sure how I did. I
> pretty much just said what was in the editorial, and Clark talked
> about morality. It was like this big impasse, with no one convincing
> anyone to change. The weird thing is that both sides want to save
> lives and think the other side is risking lives and is therefore
> immoral. Clark's is an idealistic idea, and mine is a practical one.
>
> Afterward, Al Checkers came up to me and said he's got nothing
> against me personally. I sort of smiled, and he said, "But you're
> preaching sin, and you've got to give that up. It's poisonous, what
> you're doing, against God." Then he said, "I like you, Jamie, and
> God loves you. But God hates the sin in you. And bad things
> happen to sinners."
>
> He walked away before I could think of anything to say. But I
> saw Mrs. Buel put her hand on Al's shoulder and give him a
> friendly nod when he passed her.
>
> On the way out I went over to the refreshment table and picked
> up one of the pamphlets Mrs. Buel had put there. At first I thought
> it was from FTV, but on the back in teeny type it gives the name of
> some organization that's not even in this state. The pamphlet's full
> of lies about homosexuality, like gay people molest children and try

to "recruit" children to make them gay, and "the homosexual lifestyle" is promiscuous and against God's will and the Bible, and books and articles about homosexuality and even things like gay pride marches are attempts to "promote" homosexuality so more people, especially kids, will "become" gay. It calls homosexuality a "selfish choice of lifestyle," too. Ha! I sure didn't choose to be gay, if I am, and neither did Terry or Ernie. Who'd choose something people hate so much?

I'm not sure what it meant by "selfish," except it did say something about homosexuals not having kids—which isn't true— and having more money than straight people because they don't have kids, and I think "selfish" has something to do with that reasoning, if you can call it reasoning. You know, God wants everyone to be fruitful and multiply, maybe.

Then in a boxed-in section in different type it said, "This is the deviant lifestyle that the new health education curriculum will teach as acceptable to the children of Wilson." I think FTV must've added that to the rest of the pamphlet. It sure looked as if that boxed-in section could have been left blank for different groups to put in their own stuff.

And then when I showed the pamphlet to Mom and Dad, Mom literally turned pale. She agreed about the boxed-in section, and she said the organization whose name was in tiny type is a big national one that backs local groups, especially on school issues, and she gave Dad an I-told-you-so look, and Dad gave me the lecture again about the paper's needing to be careful.

I sure hope Ernie never sees that pamphlet or anything like it. But lots of people were reading it.

And I still didn't say anything about it. I couldn't think anymore, and I was shaking. All I could do was leave. I felt sick, like I was going to throw up.

I have to not be that way. If someone says something wrong about homosexuality, I should argue against it, just like I'd argue against anything else that was wrong. I should do that even if it's scary. When kids tell fag jokes or say "That's so gay," or say someone's dykey-looking, I never say anything. Once or twice I've walked away, but that's mostly been to hide my red face. My stomach cramps up and my hands sweat and my head sort of buzzes, and it's all because I want to say, "That's a lousy joke" or "Would you say something like that about black people?" (Actually, some of them might, though.) But I'm a coward.

Why?

I guess because I'm afraid they'll think I'm gay.

Well, aren't I? And don't some of them think that already? Brandon's sure never stopped thinking it. Al, too, I'm sure. And maybe Tessa.

Haven't I gone beyond being a Maybe?

I know I've never felt about a boy the way I feel about Tessa. I know I can't see myself married to a man or buying into all that traditional male-female stuff. I don't think I fit with that, even though I love my own family, and I think "normal" families are fine. It's just that I think being in one—being the wife and mother in one—would be wrong for me and whatever poor guy I married. A lie.

And I don't want to live a lie, even if people like Mrs. Buel think I should.

Jamie put the yellow notebook away. Then she lay down on her bed and closed her eyes.

But sleep didn't come to her till it was nearly dawn.

The next morning, remembering her promise to Terry, Jamie looked for Ernie as soon as she arrived at school, but she couldn't find him anywhere. In English, Terry said he hadn't seen him either, and at lunch, he said, "I think Ernie's cut school. And I don't want to get him in trouble with his mom by calling to make sure he's not home sick, in case he *has* cut. What I'd really like to do is go find him."

"Yeah, but how'd you know where to look?"

"I wouldn't. But I could make some good guesses."

"There's only a few more hours of school."

"Jamie, if something's really wrong . . ."

The end-of-lunch bell rang, and Terry headed down the hall to his locker. "I'm going now. Sudden stomachache," he said, "if anyone asks."

"Okay," Jamie called after him. "Good luck."

An official-looking piece of stationery headed WILSON SCHOOL COMMITTEE fluttered off Matt's desk when Jamie unlocked the newspaper office later that afternoon; Terry hadn't returned. Jamie grabbed it and was about to put it back unread when its single sentence caught her eye:

You are requested to appear before the Wilson School Committee on this Wednesday evening, October 13, to discuss your position as faculty adviser to the Wilson High Telegraph and the paper's policy, especially as regards editorials.

Jamie was just putting the letter back when Matt came in. Silently, she showed it to him. Then she said, "I probably shouldn't have read this. But it fell off your desk."

Matt took it from her. "I probably shouldn't have left it out."

"What's going on?"

Matt sat down heavily, his face creased with worry. "I'm not sure. But obviously it has to do with the condom editorial."

"Then why didn't they ask me to come?" Jamie asked angrily.

"Because you're a student and I'm a teacher."

"Well, if they're going to get mad at the paper, I want to be there!"

"I like your spirit, Jamie, and I admire your guts. But I think I ought to handle this alone."

"No," said Jamie. "I'm going to go to that meeting. They can't throw me out, can they?"

"I don't know. I suppose they can try. But it's an open meeting. I don't think there's anything in the open-meeting law that says minors can't go. But look"—he put his hand on Jamie's arm—"I have a feeling it's going to get pretty nasty. I guess I can't stop you from going, but promise me you'll clear it with your parents first?"

"Okay," Jamie said—and then Tessa burst in, waving a manila envelope and shouting, "I've got them! Our nature pictures, and they're . . ." She stopped, looking from Matt to Jamie. "What's wrong?"

"Nothing that can't wait," Matt said. "Let's see those photos."

Jamie looked over Matt's shoulder as he studied them. They were good: a red-winged blackbird flying low over the marsh, with tall grass waving in the wind; a gnarled apple tree, heavy with fruit; a big pile of raked leaves in someone's yard with two small children and a dog playing in it; a shot of lobstermen hauling traps against a stormy-looking sky . . .

"Great," said Matt when they'd gotten that far. "Autumn in Wilson. Any more harbor shots?"

Tessa flipped to the back of the pile and pulled out a photo showing a forest of masts in the yacht basin and one of a small boy rowing a punt among moored lobster boats.

"What can I say?" Matt shuffled through the rest of the pile. "Jamie, why don't you choose some for your essay, draft it, and then let me see? How about the issue after this one? Or do you think you could have it ready by this one . . ."

Matt broke off, looking through the puckered glass pane in the door, where someone was gesturing frantically.

Jamie, who was closest, got up and opened the door, revealing Terry, his jacket awry and his face pale.

"Jamie," he said under his breath. "Jamie, you've got to come. I don't want the others. Please come. It's Ernie."

Jamie nodded and went back into the room. "Emergency." She picked up her books. "I'll try for this week, Matt, and I'll be back today if I can. Meanwhile"—she shoved a manila folder toward him—"here's what I've got so far for this issue."

"Jamie . . ." Matt began.

"Sorry." With an apologetic wave, mostly toward Tessa, Jamie hurried out the door.

"What?" she said to Terry as soon as the door had closed behind them and he was hurrying her down the hall toward the main entrance. "What's happened?"

"I found him. He was on the beach; I thought he'd be there. He was just sitting, staring at the water, and he didn't say anything when I went up to him. It was weird, Jamie, really spooky. So I sat down and put my arm around him, and he started crying. It was like he'd never stop. Then he did stop, all of a sudden, and sort of smiled and said, 'I'm sorry. I'm okay now.' He wouldn't say anything more than that, but I got him to get into my car, and . . ." Terry stopped; they were outside now, on the school steps. "And he said he was hungry, can you believe it? So I said okay, we'll get something to eat, and I asked him if he'd mind if you came along and he said he wouldn't. I'm scared, Jamie; he's acting so weird."

"He wouldn't have taken anything, would he?"

"I don't think so. I don't know for sure, but it wouldn't be like him. He's so careful of his body, because of swimming. I don't think so. Here. My car's over here."

Terry led Jamie to the far end of the parking lot, where his car was parked under some low-hanging trees.

It was empty.

"Oh, no," Terry groaned. "Oh, God. Ernie!" he called. "Ernie!" He glanced frantically around the lot.

"Wait, Terry," Jamie said. "Let's think. It's a warm afternoon. He could just have decided to go for a walk, or . . ."

"Or the pool!" Terry exclaimed. "There's another meet this Saturday; if he was feeling better, he might have decided to work out. Sometimes when he's depressed he swims. 'Swimming it off,' he calls it. He said once it was better than Prozac—not that he takes Prozac; I think he was kidding. But he does get depressed. Come on." Terry grabbed Jamie's hand and pulled her toward the gym.

"But wouldn't there be other kids practicing? If there's a meet . . ."

"It's too late. They don't have a long practice on Mondays."

Terry hurried Jamie into the building and through the hall to the pool entrance. The damp, acrid smell of chlorine hit Jamie's nostrils as soon as Terry opened the door—and she heard the rhythmic sound of someone swimming . . .

"It's him," Terry whispered, sinking down into one of the stadium seats. "He's doing laps. Oh, Jamie, look at him! Thank God he's okay."

"Yes," said Jamie. "Hey, I was sure he would be. I bet he's a lot tougher than you think."

Terry gave her an odd look, but he didn't say anything.

"Aren't you going to let him know we're here?"

"Nope. I'm going to let him swim it off. And then when he's finished, I'm going to tell him how great he looked out there. And then I'm going to take him to get something to eat, if he still wants that, and on the way I'm going to try to get him to talk to me." He leaned over and kissed Jamie's cheek. "Thank you, friend."

"No problem." Jamie got up. "I'll make your excuses to Matt. Just—do you think you could finish that feature on the football coach by deadline?"

"Along with the story about last Saturday's game? Yeah. Yeah, they'll be done. I'll tell the reporter to have the game piece tomorrow, okay? I'm doing the coach one, and it'll take me a little longer; I haven't interviewed him yet." Terry's eyes were still on Ernie, who was swimming steadily, smoothly, his body making hardly a ripple as it glided through the aquamarine water.

"Okay." Jamie inclined her head toward the pool. "You're right that he's beautiful when he's swimming."

"He's beautiful when he isn't swimming, too."

Jamie squeezed Terry's shoulder. "Take it easy. Call me tonight if you want, okay?"

"Yeah, okay. And, Jamie—thanks again."

E I G H T

The more Jamie thought about it, the more she thought the newspaper staff, at least the editors, should go to the school committee meeting to support Matt. The others, including Nomi, agreed when she broached it to them Tuesday, and so on Wednesday night, Jamie, Terry, Nomi, Cindy, and Tessa, along with Jack representing the reporters, all squeezed into the back row of the room in which the committee met. Morris Just, an athletic-looking middle-aged man with a neatly trimmed, graying beard, looked surprised, as did the other committee members at the conference table in front of the room, but no one asked the newspaper staff to leave. Matt, sitting uncomfortably next to a pleasant-looking plump woman in the second row, also looked surprised; then he scribbled a note and passed it to them. "I don't believe you guys," it said. "Thanks. Please be careful."

The plump woman turned around and smiled at them, and Tessa whispered, "I wonder if that's Mrs. Caggin."

"It is," Cindy whispered back. "She used to be my Brownie leader. She's a neat lady."

There was a long agenda, and Jamie found herself tuning out during much of it. But finally Mr. Just cleared his throat and said, "Next is the matter of the school paper—the editorial policy. Lisa?"

Jamie felt her heart speed up, and she leaned forward.

"Thank you," said Mrs. Buel. "I'm sure the paper means well. I know how worked up high school kids can get over certain issues, and I think it's wonderful when kids today are enthusiastic. But it's up to adults to channel their enthusiasm and provide guidance. I'm just not sure that's being done as well as it could be where the school paper is concerned, and I think the first issue's editorial was a case in point . . ."

"You mean the condom editorial?" interrupted a large, jowly man sitting next to Mr. Just. "Very sensible, I thought."

"That's a matter of opinion," said another committee member, a slender woman in green—"Mrs. Grasshopper," Tessa whispered; Jamie suppressed a laugh. "I think we should hear Lisa out."

"The editorial's over and done with," Mrs. Buel said. "What we have to concern ourselves with is the future, and that's why I suggested we invite Matt Caggin to our meeting . . ."

"Invite!" muttered Jack. "Wasn't it more like a summons?"

". . . to discuss his position as adviser and to tell us what the paper's policy is regarding editorials."

"Matt?" Mr. Just peered at him over the top of a sheaf of papers he'd been thumbing through. "Why don't you tell us about the paper's policy?"

Matt got up and strode to the front of the room, where he stood on one side, between the school committee and the audience. Mrs. Caggin turned slightly toward him in her seat.

"I'd be glad to tell you about the paper's policy," he said. "We're very proud of it at Wilson High, and I'm very proud of my staff, many of whom were concerned enough about this matter to come tonight. No, I didn't ask them to come. They decided that on their own." He smiled at them briefly, then turned back to the committee. "Our policy is simple. The editor in chief writes editorials and may invite staff members, faculty, or students to write op-ed pieces. The editorials the editor writes don't necessarily reflect the views of the staff as a whole, but like everything else in the paper, they do have to be approved by the faculty adviser, who, as you know, is me."

Mr. Just raised his hand. "Excuse, me, Matt. What's your standard for approving an editorial? I mean, when an editor shows you an editorial, what do you look for?"

"I look for accuracy and style, mostly."

"Not subject matter?" asked Mrs. Buel, twiddling a pencil.

"Only in that I make sure the subject matter is pertinent— that it has something to do with a school issue or a local one, or, occasionally, a national issue about which the school community is concerned."

"You don't look for its appropriateness, its suitability for young, impressionable minds?"

Matt's voice tightened, and Jamie saw Mrs. Caggin's mouth tense. "We're talking about high school students here, Mrs. Buel, not children. If an editorial were obscene or libelous or, possibly, frivolous, I'd veto it. But . . ."

"So you do have veto power," Mrs. Buel interrupted. "Have you ever exercised it? I believe you've been the paper's adviser for several years?"

"Eight," Matt said; Jamie could see that he was getting angry. "And no, I've never used it."

"Don't you think," Mrs. Buel asked, "that the paper has an obligation to reflect the moral standards of the community?"

"Of which community?"

"Of Wilson."

"No, I don't, not in its editorials. Not of Wilson, the town, and not always of the high school community either. Besides, I'm not sure either community has a single set of standards. A newspaper isn't in the business of setting or reflecting standards anyway; it's in the business of reporting the news. The *Telegraph* has a responsibility to report on controversial issues and to reflect all opinions, insofar as that's possible given the limited resources of a school paper."

"Ah," said Mrs. Buel triumphantly. "But the editorial in question didn't do that. It just 'reflected,' as you put it, one person's opinion, that of the editor."

"That," Matt spat out angrily, "is what an editorial is supposed to do! An editorial *is* opinion! Anyone who disagrees with what's expressed in an editorial or in anything else, for that matter, can write a letter to the editor."

"But, Matt," said Mr. Just, "I believe the paper often does have an op-ed page, and I think many papers request op-ed pieces from the opposing side when there's an editorial on one side of a hot issue."

Jamie jumped to her feet. "We did request one. And I—I'm Jamie Crawford, the editor in chief, and I wrote the editorial that Mrs. Buel is upset about. I did talk to someone about doing an op-ed piece on the other side, but that person ended up not writing it. I asked a lot of other people, too, but no one wanted to do it, and then it was too late. There weren't any opposing letters to the editor for the next issue; we were sure there'd be some. But obviously no one was upset enough to write one."

"Or," said Mrs. Buel with a thin smile, "perhaps no one dared write one, given the fact that everyone must know editorials need faculty approval and given the fact that the other side wasn't represented fairly in the paper."

Nomi stood up beside Jamie. "I'm the one who Jamie asked to write the op-ed piece. And I talked about it and thought about it and everything, but I'm not a writer and I—well, I guess I was scared . . ."

"Oh?" Mrs. Buel raised her eyebrows. "Scared? Of what, dear?"

"Well, most kids are for the condom distribution, and I'm sure the school administration approves of it, since it's the nurse who's handing them out. So I—well, I guess I didn't want to—you know."

Mrs. Buel leaned forward. "Were you afraid of some kind of retaliation if you wrote the op-ed piece?"

Nomi looked confused. "What? I don't . . ."

"Were you afraid you'd lose friends or be harassed or asked to leave the paper's staff?"

"No," said Nomi, clearly astonished. "No, of course not, I . . . Um—I was scared of not being able to say it right, I guess, and of being in the minority. But I didn't think anyone would *do* anything to me or anything." She turned to Jamie. "Jamie, I'm sorry I didn't write it, really I am."

"It's okay," Jamie said softly. "Nomi is our art editor," she explained to the committee. "She's a better writer than she thinks she is, but she's always been sort of reluctant to write. Anyway, if there's any fault here, it's mine, not Matt's."

Mrs. Caggin, Jamie could see, was smiling faintly.

Mrs. Buel raised her eyebrows again. "Matt's? You mean Mr. Caggin's, don't you? Are you in the habit of calling Mr. Caggin by his first name?"

"Oh, for heaven's sake, Lisa," Matt said. "We're very informal on the newspaper. We have to be; it's a high-stress job, especially since we all have other responsibilities."

"You took on the job of faculty adviser to the paper, Mr. Caggin," said Mrs. Buel. "If it's too much for you, I suggest you let the administration know." She turned toward her colleagues on the committee. "The point is that there is no place for this kind of laxity at our high school. High school students are at the period in their development during which they will either become responsible, morally upright citizens or irresponsible, morally selfish ones. We tend to forget that they're still children, in need of our moral guidance . . ."

"Yes, Lisa," interrupted Mr. Just. "We do know how you feel about that issue."

The jowly man nodded as if he agreed, but two or three other committee members, who'd been silent so far, looked annoyed, and they'd smiled at Mrs. Buel's words.

A woman in a red suit, who'd been sitting quietly in the front row, stood up and faced the other audience members. "I'm Laura Hodges." (Jamie, thinking of Karen and Sam and their association with Brandon, groaned inwardly.) "Those of you who go to Lord's Assembly know me, as do my neighbors on Partridge Road, as do PTA people. I have a daughter at the high school and a son at the middle school. The school committee may know how Lisa Buel feels, but many others do not and are not aware of the problems she's found in our education system. That is why we've formed FTV, Families for Traditional Values, and I must say, we've enjoyed a gratifying amount of support already. I, for one, was appalled at the school's condom policy and at the editorial supporting it, and many people we've contacted were—are—also appalled. I don't really blame you, dear," she said to Jamie. "You were fired up, but you needed guidance to steer your thinking into more acceptable lines. I don't know what Mr. Caggin was thinking, or your parents, I'm sure."

Jamie, who felt ready to explode, burst out, "My parents! My parents have nothing to do with this! And I don't see why I need guidance just because I wrote my opinion, which in this country I have every right to do!"

"Right on, Jamie," said Terry, and Jack, Cindy, and Tessa started to clap.

Several others in the audience followed suit, but Mr. Just held up his hand. "Ladies and gentlemen, please. Mrs. Hodges, do you have anything more to say?"

"Yes. I have here"—she whipped out a piece of paper—"a petition for Mr. Caggin's removal from his position as newspaper adviser, signed by all the members of FTV."

There was a muted gasp from the front row—Mrs. Caggin, Jamie was sure—and in the stunned silence that followed, Mrs. Hodges handed the paper to Mr. Just.

"Thank you," he said evenly. "We'll take it under advisement. Does anyone else have anything more to say on this issue?"

Jamie searched desperately for a reply, but could think of nothing. Nomi looked as if she was about to cry, Jack looked furious, and Tessa, Terry, and Cindy seemed to be in shock. Jamie couldn't see Matt's face, but she could see the tension in his back and shoulders.

"All right," said Mr. Just. "Then I think we on the committee need to go into executive session in order to discuss this further. For any of you not familiar with the open-meeting law," he went on, "a town board's meetings must always be open to the public, except when the board goes into executive session, which can be held when there's a sensitive personnel matter to discuss. I believe the only other things on tonight's agenda are the health text review and the question of condom distribution. Let's dispose of those, if we can. Lisa, you're on again."

"Health text?" whispered Cindy. "And condoms? What's going on?"

"I don't know," Jamie whispered back. "But I think we're about to find out." She put her hand on Nomi's arm. "Nom', it's not your fault. Like I said, if it's anyone's, it's mine . . ."

"Shh!" Terry tipped his head toward Mrs. Buel.

". . . so I think," she was saying, "that since the texts used in the high school's health classes include positive material about matters that are unacceptable to a large segment of the community, we should review them carefully with an eye to choosing different ones. I'd like to propose that the texts be collected at the next meeting of each health class and held until a book review committee, which I'll be glad to form and to chair, has had a chance to study them and compare them with others that are available. I'd also like to propose that the committee look further into the advisability of making condoms available to high school students."

"Lisa, could you outline your objections to the current texts?" asked the grasshoppery-looking woman.

"Certainly," said Mrs. Buel. "The section on AIDS, for example, in the senior text, devotes three paragraphs and a very graphic diagram to condoms and only a couple of sentences to abstinence. Again, high school students are at a sensitive, impressionable age, especially as regards sexual matters. They need guidance in order to help them make healthy decisions about their lives, and they certainly shouldn't be encouraged to have premarital sex; condom availability encourages that— as does the text. For example, the section on lifestyles says, and I quote: 'More and more couples these days are choosing to live together before marrying.' It also says, 'Gay and lesbian couples in some parts of the country can register as domestic partners and can adopt children; some opt to have children of their own.' These are just samples, mind you, of material that we find objectionable and misleading. Children tend to think anything they read in a book is the truth, is acceptable, and that of course is not the case."

"High school students are not . . ." Matt burst out, but the grasshoppery woman interrupted, clucking her tongue. "Pretty revealing samples, if you ask me. I'm glad you brought them to our attention, Lisa. I agree that we should review the question of condoms and also the high school health texts, and perhaps those used on other levels as well."

"Oh, hang on, Helen," the jowly man said to her. "Lisa, you, too. There's nothing inaccurate about those statements in the text. They're statements of fact."

"Statements of fact without guidance are misleading and irresponsible," Lisa Buel retorted. "Condoms encourage promiscuity. It is illegal to be homosexual in many states; homosexuals are mentally unbalanced; they get and spread disease; they molest children. Where are those facts?"

"Where indeed?" said the grasshoppery woman.

"The act of sodomy is illegal in some states," said Matt. "Not homosexuality. Heterosexuals can commit sodomy, and many do. The American Psychological Association and the American Psychiatric Association long ago removed homosexuality from their lists of mental disorders. Heterosexuals as well as homosexuals get and spread disease, and many more heterosexuals than homosexuals molest children. And condoms can prevent disease and pregnancy. If we're talking about facts, Lisa, let's get them right."

Lisa Buel smirked slightly. "I wonder what your interest is in this, Mr. Caggin. As I recall, you teach English, not health."

"And I'm also the paper's adviser," Matt said hotly. "As such, I have to be informed about issues that involve the school, and I also . . ."

"That's enough," said Mr. Just. "I'm reluctant to let this review business go forward, because I'm afraid of its turning into some kind of vendetta. But I suppose we'd better do it to satisfy those who are concerned." He turned to the other committee members. "Discussion?"

"I'm not happy with it either," said the jowly man. "But I agree that we'd better let these people pursue it, if there really are complaints."

"Oh, there are, there are," said Lisa Buel. "I've been talking with people, and the more they become aware of what's been going on, the more dissatisfaction they feel."

"I never knew," said Karen Hodges's mother, "what was in that new health education curriculum till Lisa brought it to my attention."

"That's odd," commented a woman from the back row. "It was publicized in the town paper, and there were copies of it available in the library."

"And a good many people in town trusted the school committee and the school itself to institute only responsible courses," Mrs. Hodges retorted. "It took Lisa to show us that wasn't so, and I for one thank God she was elected."

"Ladies, please," said Mr. Just. "Let's put it to a vote. Someone make a motion."

The jowly man moved that Mrs. Buel be empowered to form a committee to study the textbooks and the question of condom distribution, and Mrs. Buel amended the motion to add that the books and condoms be removed and withheld at least till the study's completion.

"The motion passes as amended," Mr. Just announced after a show of hands. "Now, it's late, and we still need to resolve Matt's situation. Non-committee members, you're excused. Matt, you may stay for a few minutes if you have anything to say to us in private."

Matt shook his head. "I'd rather have a chance to speak after your decision. I've already made my basic point."

"Very well, then." Mr. Just stood up. "Thank you all for coming. School committee members, we'll take a five-minute break and then return for executive session."

About half an hour later, while Jamie, Terry, Nomi, Jack, Cindy, and Tessa waited with Matt and Mrs. Caggin in the hall, sitting on the floor and playing twenty questions to pass the time, Morris Just called Matt into the meeting room. And a few minutes after that, Matt came back out. "The good news," he said, taking his wife's hand, "is that I can continue as adviser. The bad news is that editorials have to give equal weight to all sides of any controversial issue."

"That's ridiculous!" Jamie shouted. "That means they won't be editorials at all."

"I know. I asked if they'd let us run real editorials whenever we're able to get an op-ed, but they refused that on the grounds that we didn't with the condom issue. We don't have a choice, gang, at least not now."

The next morning a notice went up outside the nurse's office saying condoms would no longer be available, until further notice. In health class, the teacher collected all the textbooks. Almost everyone cheered, but Jamie felt a cold knot in the pit of her stomach, and Terry, across from her in the next row, looked grim.

N I N E

Terry slammed his tray down on the newspaper table at lunch that same day; Jack was there, plus all the editors, including Nomi. "We do have a choice, blast it!" Terry exploded. "We can't let them silence us."

"What's that AIDS bumper sticker?" Jamie said. "*Silence Is Death?* Something like that."

"Yeah," Jack said. "It sure applies here, too."

Cindy, her gray baseball cap askew, bit fiercely into an oozing tuna sandwich. "Aren't we supposed to have free speech in this country?" she said when she'd swallowed. "Freedom of the press? We ought to be able to say what we want to say in spite of the stupid school committee. Maybe we could sort of, you know, bend their rules."

"I wish." Terry pulled out a chair and sat down. "But how do you not reflect all sides and look as if you are? I'm only a sports editor, but I can't make a win look like a loss, and that's what it would take. It's not possible."

"No, it isn't," Jamie said quietly. "Maybe we just shouldn't run editorials at all for a while."

"Maybe," said Cindy, "we shouldn't run a paper at all."

Tessa grimaced. "That would be giving in to them. What we should do, maybe, is another paper. A different one."

They all stared at her.

"Cool," Jack said admiringly. "I wonder if we could."

"Yeah." Cindy gave Tessa a friendly poke on the shoulder. "That's a neat idea." Then she frowned. "But wouldn't that get Matt in trouble?"

"Not," Jamie said slowly, "if the new paper had nothing to do with him."

Nomi pushed her tray away and scraped her chair back, standing as if about to leave. She'd barely returned Jamie's tentative but hopeful "Hi" right before the bell in homeroom, and hadn't looked at her in the two morning classes they shared.

"Hey, Nom'." Jamie put her hand on Nomi's arm. "You haven't eaten anything. You okay?"

Nomi nodded.

"No, you're not," said Terry. "Come on. Give."

Nomi burst into quiet tears. "Don't you guys see?" she said, sobbing. "It really *is* all my fault. If I'd written that stupid op-ed . . ."

Jamie stood up quickly and hugged her; Nomi stiffened. "You couldn't have known what would happen, Nomi." Jamie moved out of the hug and studied Nomi's face. "Hey, who knows? It might have happened anyway."

"Yeah." Cindy handed Nomi a tissue. "I think the school committee's out to get us no matter what we do. Out to get Matt, anyway, especially that Buel woman."

"No one blames you, Nomi." Tessa pushed Nomi's tray forward. "Come on, girl, sit down and eat. We can't have you fainting from hunger. We've got plans to make." She looked at Terry, then at Jamie. "Don't we?"

"I don't know." Jamie sat down again. "Do we?"

"We could go ahead with the old *Telegraph* and publish another paper, too," Terry suggested. "That'd keep Matt out of it."

"I like it," Cindy said eagerly. "Wow, what genius!" She swept her cap off her head and bowed from her seat, first to Tessa, then to Terry.

"We couldn't use the school print shop, though," Jack said.

"Good point," Jamie agreed. "We'd have to keep the school completely out of it. We could distribute it here, I think, but we couldn't print it here or write it here or anything."

"Have we got enough news for two papers?" asked Tessa. "I mean, I can always take plenty of pictures, but there's only a limited amount of stuff happening."

"How about just opinion?" Jamie suggested, her excitement growing. "It's true there might not be enough news for two papers. But if the renegade paper . . ."

"Good name!" said Terry. "The *Renegade Telegraph*—that's great!"

Cindy grinned. "I have a funny feeling FTV isn't going to like this much. Or the school administration."

"But if we don't do it on school property or with school materials," Jack said, "how do we do it?"

"He's got a point, Jamie," said Terry. "It'll be pretty tricky if we can't use school stuff."

"Yes, but a couple of us have computers at home. And you've got a scanner, too, or your parents do, anyway. We'll self-publish. Look," Jamie went on, "we could do it like an old-fashioned broadside. They were more like bulletins than newspapers, and they dealt with one subject, usually. We'll stick to opinion, not news, unless the news is, I don't know, pertinent. And we'll all write it," she added, looking significantly at each of them in turn. "I don't want it to be just a vehicle for me, even if it is opinion. And we'll do it right. Each piece can really represent its own view, none of this weak stuff they're looking for." She glanced around the table. Nomi had sat back down, but she hadn't said a word, and although she still wasn't eating, she was looking at her lunch tray instead of at the rest of them.

"Nom'?" Jamie asked gently. "What do you think?"

Nomi started, then said, "Huh? About—about another paper? I—I just . . ." She got up before anyone could stop her and bolted past the teacher-monitor, who looked up with a startled expression and then looked down again as Nomi fled out the door.

"Oh, my," said Terry.

Everyone looked at Jamie.

"I don't know what's wrong with her. It can't just be that she feels responsible for the trouble we're in."

"Right," Tessa said. "Maybe she doesn't trust our opinions about much of anything to be the same as hers. I mean, we do all sort of feel the same way about most things, you know? But she doesn't."

"Maybe she should start her own paper," Terry said angrily.

"She's entitled to her opinion," Jamie said, trying to make light of it. "I'd be sorry to lose her. Cindy, I bet you could fill in as art editor until she decides—do layout, anyway; you've already done a great job helping Nomi lay out ads."

Cindy looked pleased. "Thanks," she said. "Okay."

"Nomi's suffering," Tessa said. "And so are you," she added softly to Jamie.

Jamie knew Tessa was right, on both counts. She felt a hard place in her throat, as if all her pain over losing Nomi's friendship were stuck there.

"Okay," Jack said briskly, breaking the silence. "Okay. So we do two papers, one regular and one just opinion. The thing is, Jamie, if we do that, what'll there be left over for you to write about in the *Telegraph* for editorials?"

"Let's see," Jamie began, trying to pull herself into the discussion. "Um . . ."

"Oh, there's plenty," Terry said, glancing at her sympathetically. "The shortage of soap in the boys' bathroom, right, Jack? Now that's a real stunner. I bet you guys don't know about that."

"Really?" said Cindy. "Don't be so sure. There's a similar shortage in the girls' bathroom."

"Yeah," Tessa put in. "And the little soap that's there is really harsh. It's murder on your skin." She made her eyes big and round. "Something needs to be done . . ."

"On the other hand . . ." said Terry.

Cindy groaned, and Jamie managed a feeble smile.

"On the other hand," Terry continued, "it's important to have clean hands . . ."

"Even," Tessa put in, "if there's no skin on them. You could interview the nurse, Jamie."

"Right," said Jack, "and Mr. Zemma in auto shop. I don't think he knows what soap is, so maybe he's got some ideas about it being more healthy not to wash."

Terry snapped his fingers. "Geeze, right! There's a potential op-ed there, so I bet it's really a *Telegraph* subject."

Jamie laughed. "Okay," she said as the bell rang. "I guess there'll always be plenty of stuff to write about in the old *Telegraph*."

Jamie called Nomi that night to see if she was all right and to ask if she wanted to work on the *Renegade*.

"Thanks for calling," Nomi said evenly—cautiously, too, Jamie thought. "Yes, I'm okay, and no, I think I'd better stick to the *Telegraph*." Her voice caught a little then as she added, "Jamie, I'm sorry. I just think you're so wrong. I'm just—I'm sad for you."

"Sad?" Jamie asked, astonished. "Why sad, Nom'?"

"It's wrong," Nomi whispered. "What you believe, what the others believe. And what you—what you're doing, I guess. It's so very wrong. I'm afraid your *Renegade* paper's going to be a vehicle for that, for those things."

"But, Nomi, we—what things, for Pete's sake?"

"I've got to go, Jamie. Goodbye."

Before she could object, Jamie heard a click and the line went dead.

Jamie bought paper for the *Renegade Telegraph*, and they designed the first issue on Terry's computer, with Cindy's help. Cindy surprised them all—herself, too, she told them—by drawing a really good cartoon for the first issue, showing the Wilson High *Telegraph* office and staff in chains. And they all tossed around ideas for stories, finally ending up with two short articles, announcements really, on one side of a single sheet. "Like a broadside," Jamie said again. They put Cindy's cartoon, thanks to Terry's scanner, on the other side, and they decided to print 400 copies. There were about 350 students in the school, so that would be enough for faculty as well, with a few left over.

By late Friday afternoon, when the *Renegade* began bouncing out of Terry's printer, Jamie felt as if she'd suddenly been freed of binding chains like those in Cindy's cartoon.

THE RENEGADE TELEGRAPH

Published occasionally, independently of the Wilson High *Telegraph*

Renegade Founded

The *Renegade Telegraph* has been founded as a journal of opinion by the Wilson High *Telegraph* staff, to fill a gap opened by the recent school committee ruling on editorials. In that ruling, made on October 13, it was decreed that all editorials had to present all sides of every subject. "The *Telegraph* has always tried to balance editorials on its op-ed page and/or on its letters pages," said Jamie Crawford, editor of the Wilson High paper. "But it is in the nature of an editorial to be persuasive. The new ruling fails to recognize that. We founded the *Renegade* in order to be able to continue publishing honest opinion."

Editorial

In its recent action to muzzle the Wilson High *Telegraph* and to "study" the school's health texts, the school committee appears to be embarking on a dangerous and repressive course. Freedom of speech and of the press applies to schools as well as to the community at large; the sooner the school committee admits that and retracts its decision, the better.

Renegade *staff: Jamie Crawford, Terry Gage, Tessa Gillespie, Jack Kellog, and Cindy Nash. The* Renegade *will be published as needed, whenever the* Telegraph *is unable to explore a vital issue honestly and thoroughly. With that in mind, we may do some investigative pieces, and from time to time we may cover news as well.*

"Pretty good first issue for a simple broadside," Terry said, stacking the sheets neatly as they came out of the printer. Tessa, Cindy, and Jack had already left, and Terry, though he had worked as hard as the rest of them, had seemed preoccupied all afternoon. "I can't wait for Monday," he said with what sounded to Jamie like forced enthusiasm, or maybe sarcasm.

"I can." Jamie read through the *Renegade* for the hundredth time, trying to imagine how Matt would react, her parents, the principal, Lisa Buel. "But I'm glad we did it. I think I am, anyway."

"I also can't wait till Monday," Terry said, sitting on the edge of the table, "because I won't see Ernie till then."

"How come?"

"He had some news for me this morning," Terry told her, with what Jamie recognized as false casualness. "He's decided to see if he can be straight. He asked Vicky Chase out."

"*What?*" Jamie asked, stunned.

"You heard me. Vicky Chase." He laughed sardonically. "He thinks if anyone can make him straight, she can."

Jamie hardly knew how to react. "At least Vicky's kind," she said slowly. "I don't think she's homophobic or anything. And if he really *is* gay . . ."

"It's okay, Jamie." Terry slid off the table and turned his back to her, picking up the finished papers and putting them in the box they were planning to take to school early Monday morning. "Thanks. It's okay."

Jamie touched his shoulder. "It's not okay. And I'm—Oh, Terry."

For Terry had turned then, clinging tightly to Jamie for an anguished moment before breaking away and leaving the room.

TEN

Saturday morning, in the middle of a breakfast-table argument about why neither set of parents would let Ronnie and his friend Fred sleep out in the woods without an adult, the phone rang. Jamie, glad to be out of the line of fire, ran to answer it.

"I just realized," Tessa said without preamble as soon as Jamie had answered, "that you've never been to my house and I've never been to yours, and I think we ought to fix that up right away, since we're going to be working together on those essays plus on both papers. You could come here this morning and I could go there this afternoon, or the other way around. Okay?"

Jamie felt a smile steal over her face even as she warned herself that there was probably no special significance to the invitation. "Okay. Sure."

"Great! You want to come here first?"

"Sure."

Tessa chuckled. "Will you say 'sure' again if I say come now?"

Jamie laughed. "Sure," she said. "Be right there. Robert Road, right? Which house?"

Less than half an hour later, Jamie parked her bike outside a neat gray shingle house with green shutters, well back from the narrow street, in a fenced-in, carefully tended yard. A pile of leaves filled one corner, and Tessa, looking almost ordinary in jeans and a yellow-and-green-plaid shirt, was raking more leaves toward it; Jamie saw that her nails were free of polish, although the tiny star still glittered in her nose. A small pig-tailed girl played with a kitten nearby, scooping up leaves with her hand and tossing them gently at the kitten.

Tessa put down her rake. "Angela, come meet my new friend."

The little girl picked up the kitten and slipped one hand in Tessa's as Tessa walked toward Jamie. "Hi," Tessa said, smiling.

"Hi to you, too," Jamie said. "And hi, Angela. Hello, kitten." She stroked the kitten's tiny head with her forefinger; it purred instantly, loudly.

"You're Jamie," Angela said. "Tessa told us. This is Golly." She indicated the kitten.

"Golly?" Jamie looked at Tessa over the top of Angela's head.

"Yep." Tessa wiggled Angela's hand, still in her own. "Tell Jamie why."

"Well, the first time Daddy heard Golly purr, he said, 'Golly, what a purr,' so we thought that would be the right name."

"I see," Jamie said gravely. "It's a cute name. And she's a cute kitty."

"He," said Angela. "Golly's a boy."

"Golly, I wouldn't have guessed that," Jamie said, and Angela giggled.

"His name really works." With the kitten, she twirled away from Tessa, back to the leaves.

"Don't you mess up my pile, Angie!" Tessa called after her. "Come see inside," she said to Jamie. "Come see my room."

Jamie followed her up the flagstone path and onto the front steps.

Tessa pushed the door open. "Mom," she called. "Jamie's here."

A tall, pleasant-looking woman wearing a bright red smock came into the front hall from the back of the house, a plastic bag of white pebbles in her hand. She looked like an adult version of Tessa, except her eyes were set wider apart, her face was fuller, and she had none of Tessa's flamboyance. "Hello, Jamie," she said, wiping her other hand on her smock and then holding it out. "I've been planting bulbs, first outside, now inside, to force them. You know, crocuses and paper-whites."

"Hi." Jamie shook the offered hand. "My mom does that, too."

Mrs. Gillespie's smile broadened. "The funny thing is that the people who sold us the house couldn't remember where they'd planted bulbs, so goodness knows what we're going to find come spring. I've already run into a few, planting."

"Yeah," Jamie told her. "I think I remember lots of flowers around this house in the spring. I ride by here on my bike sometimes."

"Well, I hope you ride by even more often now. Tessa's told us lots about you, all good."

"*Most* all good," Tessa corrected. "Don't want you to get stuck up."

"There's no chance of that, I'm sure," Mrs. Gillespie said graciously. "Listen, I've got to get back to work, but there's coffee in the pot in the kitchen, Tess, and the water's still hot for tea. There's about half that coffee cake left, too."

Tessa grimaced, as if her mother always offered food to people. "Jamie's probably just had breakfast, Mom."

"Probably, but if she stays as long as I hope she does, she won't have just had breakfast," Mrs. Gillespie retorted. "And if it's not quite time for lunch, she might want a little something. Do stay for lunch, Jamie, unless you girls decide to go out someplace. Okay?"

"Okay," Jamie said. "Thank you."

Mrs. Gillespie nodded and went back down the hall.

"I like your mother," Jamie said, following Tessa up the carpeted stairs to the second floor.

"Yeah." Tessa paused outside a closed door with a small grapevine wreath on it. "She'd feed the whole world if she could. It's a good thing we're all skinny in my family, because if any of us went on a diet, I think she'd die. Come on in."

Tessa's room was large, flooded with sun from two windows. A single bed, its bright multicolored spread matching the curtains, was under one of the windows, with a night table beside it. The second window was opposite a large table with a fluorescent tube running across it on a frame. Boxes of slides lined a shelf above the table, with a small projector in one corner; oversized photo books were piled on the bookcase nearby, and 4×6 file boxes filled another shelf. There were no piles of clothes draped over the chair that faced the table or on the one in the corner by the small white dresser on which a bottle or two of cologne shared space with a box of filters and a light meter. Tessa's camera bag was dangling from a door that Jamie assumed led into a closet; two old-looking cameras sat on the night table along with a lamp and the senior English textbook. Neatly framed photos marched across the walls, most of them black-and-white, but a few in color.

"I'd never guess," Jamie said, "that you were planning to be a ballet dancer."

Tessa grinned. "That's good. I'm so relieved! I wasn't sure the disguise would work."

Jamie noticed the red cape hanging on the closet door. "Is that a disguise, too?" she asked, and when Tessa looked startled, she added, "I noticed you took off the nail polish."

Tessa tossed her head evasively. "Oh, that," she said. "Yes. Kevin Allen called last night and asked if I was still wearing purple polish and my nose star, and I said no, just the star, so then I decided I'd better get rid of it, the polish, I mean. Along with him, you know?"

"Don't you like him anymore?" Jamie asked uncomfortably.

Tessa shrugged. "Like I said before, he's not here, and he never was very interesting. Plus, like I said, too, I don't have time." She regarded Jamie almost coquettishly. "Jack's kind of cute, though, but he's Cindy's. I don't believe in taking other people's boyfriends. Anyway"—she picked up a small vase of dried flowers and raised it in front of Jamie—"to independent womanhood, remember?"

"Right," Jamie said, glad Tessa had finally given her something she could react to openly. She seized a mug of pencils from Tessa's desk. "To independent womanhood." She gestured toward the tiny star in Tessa's nose. "Is that part of independent womanhood?" she asked shyly.

"Sort of," Tessa said. "Independence, anyway. I had this Indian friend, from India, you know? She had one and I really liked it, so she took me to have my nose done. I was only in seventh grade, and I really wanted to be different." She paused. "Aren't you going to ask if it hurts and how it feels when I have a cold? Most people do. But you're not most people, are you?"

"No, I guess not," Jamie said. Then she laughed. "But does it? Hurt?"

Tessa laughed, too. "Nope. I'm used to it, like it's part of me. Even when I have a cold. I forget it's there most of the time. But I take it out sometimes, like earrings, you know?"

They spent the rest of the morning in Tessa's room and in her basement darkroom, where Tessa showed Jamie how to develop film, and they had an enormous salad and homemade bread with Mrs. Gillespie and Angela. Mr. Gillespie, his wife explained, was working.

"Your mother," Jamie said, pushing her bike beside Tessa as they walked to Jamie's house after lunch, "has got to be one of the nicest people I've ever met."

"Well," Tessa said, "she *is* my mother."

Jamie punched her lightly. Tessa punched her lightly back, and Jamie realized that gay or not gay, it felt good to be making friends with a girl again.

Tessa seemed as intrigued with Jamie's room as Jamie had been with Tessa's. "Now see," she said when she'd glanced quickly around at the news photos and headlines on the walls and the stacks of newspapers on the bookcase, "I'd never have guessed that you want to be an astronaut. That must be what made us become friends, our uncanny talent for disguises."

"When you work for the CIA," said Jamie, "you have to be good at disguises."

"Darn!" Tessa snapped her fingers. "CIA? But it's the FBI I work for!"

"Oh, no!" Jamie cried in mock horror, falling back onto a chair. "Not the FBI!"

"Well," said Tessa, "I'm ready for a change anyway. Maybe I'll quit, see if the CIA will take me. But," she added, peering into Jamie's mirror, "I'll have to change how I look. Dye my skin, maybe, or shave off my hair."

Without thinking, Jamie said, "No, don't"—and felt her face grow hot when Tessa gave her a penetrating look.

For a moment, they both froze, and then Tessa, fluffing her hair with her hands and tossing her head so that her earrings danced, said, "I guess you're right. Kevin Allen would freak—if he ever saw me again, which I doubt he will," she added. "Let's think up another fantastically brilliant photo essay."

Monday morning, Jamie met Terry outside his house as he was carrying the box of *Renegade Telegraph*s to his car. He looked haggard, as if he hadn't slept. "So," she asked, "how are you? You look awful."

"Thanks so much. I feel awful. Except . . ." He hesitated.

"Except what?"

Terry set the box down on the front walk. "I went out on the boat with Dad," he said, almost shyly. "I knew I had to do something to keep from going crazy, like I knew Ernie wouldn't call, at least not till the weekend was over, and I didn't want to think about him being with Vicky. So there I am, hauling traps with Dad, and of course I'm thinking about Ernie anyway, and picturing him with Vicky, and suddenly I lose it; I start crying . . ." He stopped abruptly.

Jamie put her hand on his arm. "And your father?" she asked, dreading the answer.

But Terry shook his head. "No, Dad was wonderful. He'd figured it out already. I kept trying to stop blubbering, but I got all tangled up in the line I was handling and Dad came over and took it from me and then he said something like 'All that stuff about men not crying is a lot of bilge,' and then I just kind of blurted it out, you know, that I'm gay and that I love Ernie and that he's trying to be straight and everything. And . . ." Terry's voice dropped as if he was still amazed. "And Dad put his arms around me and said he wasn't surprised, that he loves me, that he's wondered for years and had sort of accepted it long ago, and that he'd been waiting for me to tell him. Then he dropped the line he was holding and we both almost fell overboard going after it and we ended up actually laughing."

"Wow!" Jamie said softly, as surprised at her own sudden envy as at Terry's father's reaction and at the fact that Terry had actually told him.

"When we told Mom," Terry went on, "she cried a little, but Dad says she just has to get used to the idea that it's really true and that she'll be all right. She really likes Ernie, so that helps, and she did seem better today." He stooped over the box again. "That's the good news. I tried to call you once, but your mom said you were with Tessa, so I decided not to bother you."

"Thank you." She watched him put the box of *Renegade*s on the back seat. "What's the bad news?" she asked when it was safely stowed.

"That I still haven't heard from Ernie. I thought he might call before school. Dumb of me, I know, but I thought he might at least tell me how it went with Vicky."

"Well, let's get going, then. Maybe you can catch him before the bell."

But Ernie wasn't in school by the time classes started, and soon Jamie's concentration shifted, for everyone was buzzing with talk about the *Renegade Telegraph*. Nomi said, a little stiffly, "It looks very nice," and Terry, meeting Jamie in the hall after he'd had social studies and she'd had Latin, said, "We're a hit!"—but he still looked haggard. That made Jamie remember Ernie.

"He's not here, right?" she asked him.

"Right. Vicky is, but I didn't trust myself to speak to her."

"Do you want me to ask her if she knows where Ernie is?"

"No. Yes. Oh, I don't know! Yes. Maybe later."

Soon afterward, though, Ernie appeared, and he and Terry vanished as soon as both had a free period. Jamie made a mental note to call Terry that night if he didn't show up at the newspaper office after school.

But Terry came back for math class and waited for Jamie in the hall afterward. "They went out twice this weekend," he told her as he and Jamie walked to the newspaper office; his voice was flat, as if he was holding back his feelings. "And he overslept this morning. He says he likes her. He says he's sorry and he doesn't want to hurt me, but she makes him feel like he could be straight. I even heard some of the guys on the swim team kidding him. Real kidding, you know, jock kidding, like they were glad to find out he's one of them after all. *Makes him feel like he could be straight!*" Terry's voice broke then and he slammed his fist against the wall; Nomi passed them, eyebrows raised, and went into the office. "Cripes, Jamie! It's not even that I'm jealous anymore. I mean, I am, but it's all wrong for him. It's like he's lying to himself, to her, to me . . ."

Jamie tried to steady him with her hands as well as with her voice. "Maybe he has to lie first before he can find out the truth. Maybe he can't accept the truth till he's figured out the lie. You've got to give him space, Terry."

"Yeah, I know, I know. But . . ."

Matt's voice, uncharacteristically harsh, cut through Terry's words. "In the office!" he shouted, striding toward them down the hall, without books or his usual after-school coffee mug. Cindy, pale and minus her perky smile, was just behind him; so was Jack. "Right now."

In Matt's hand was a copy of the *Renegade Telegraph*.

ELEVEN

Matt waved the *Renegade* as he shooed them inside, nodding perfunctorily at Nomi, who looked up, obviously startled, from the layout table. "Siddown!" he barked at the others. "Do you have any idea what's going on right now? At this very minute our esteemed principal, Mr. Bartholomew, is meeting with Mrs. Buel, several members of the school committee, and a couple of people from Mrs. Buel's little group, Families for Traditional Values, which, as you may not have figured out, is the hottest thing going in town right now. Responsible journalism in this school," he shouted, waving the *Renegade*, "does not extend to putting out a competing paper without permission." He stopped, glaring at them, his face red and his hands, Jamie saw, trembling slightly.

"It's not meant to be competing," Jamie said. "It's just . . ."

"Okay, okay." Matt sank into his chair. "Wrong word. But, Jamie, you should've known better; you've been on the paper as long as you've been in high school. You, too, Terry, and Jack also. Cindy and Tessa—where *is* Tessa?—maybe can be excused, but . . ."

Terry, glancing at Jamie, said, "Mr. Bartholomew and Mrs. Buel and everyone—they're meeting about the *Renegade*, right?"

"Yes, right. They're meeting to decide what to do about it. I was late this morning. I didn't even see your—your paper till last period . . ."

"And you're in trouble?" asked Cindy.

"Of course I'm in trouble!" Matt shouted. "How could I not be?" He took a deep breath, as if trying to calm himself. "Look," he said, as Tessa came in, "I don't think you kids have figured out what's really going on in this town."

"You mean Mrs. Buel?" Jamie asked uncomfortably.

"Yes, I mean Mrs. Buel!" Matt exclaimed. "Look," he went on, sounding patient now, as if trying to calm himself, "I think Mrs. Buel is a fanatic of sorts. A religious fanatic. Do you guys know what a theocracy is?"

"A government with a state religion," Nomi said. "Mrs. Buel's in my church. Lord's Assembly. But we don't want a religious government. We just want . . ."

"No," Matt interrupted. "No, of course *you* don't want a religious government. And I'm sure most people at Lord's Assembly don't either. But there are people who do, and Mrs. Buel, I firmly believe, is one of them. At the very least she wants everyone in Wilson to go along with her ideas about morality. Officially."

The pamphlet at Lord's Assembly, Jamie thought, disgust and anger seizing her all over again.

"Her group, too?" Terry asked. "FTV?"

"I don't know about her group. Maybe some of them, maybe all of them, maybe none of them. But I believe that Mrs. Buel wants to get as much power as she can by being on the school committee, so she can force her ideas on everyone in Wilson. We're her enemies, guys, because freedom of speech is her enemy, and so, really, is freedom of religion and all other kinds of freedoms." He paused. "Anyway, that's beside the point, sort of. Nomi, I know you're not involved, but the rest of you should've gotten permission for this paper." He thumped the *Renegade Telegraph* against his desk. "If you had, and if it had been granted, you'd be in a strong position to defend it. However, you didn't . . ."

"But," Jack protested, "we didn't use school property or school supplies."

"We did it on my family's computer," Terry explained, "with my parents' scanner, and we bought the paper . . ."

"Yes," said Matt, "as well you should have. All that was right. But what you didn't do was get permission to distribute it on school grounds."

"Is there a rule about that?" Cindy asked. "I mean, I never heard of one, and I've read the student handbook."

Matt reached into his desk drawer and pulled out a small square booklet. " 'No outside group,' " he read after thumbing through a few pages, " 'shall distribute literature, pamphlets, brochures, advertisements, or announcements on school grounds without permission of the principal.' "

"But it says outside group, Matt!" said Jamie. "We're not an outside group."

"Aren't you?" Matt asked quietly as the phone on his desk rang. "Look at the name of your paper! You know you're a renegade group, linked to the school by breaking away from it. You all work on the school paper, for Pete's sake. Matt Caggin," he said into the phone.

A moment later he said crisply, "Right," replaced the receiver, and stood up. "My turn. That was Mr. Bartholomew's secretary. I'm wanted in the office."

"Oh, no, Matt," Jamie said miserably, standing also. "I'm sorry. Shouldn't I come, too?"

"I think," Matt said grimly, his hand on the door, "that your turn will come soon enough."

It did, although not as quickly as Jamie had anticipated. For the rest of the afternoon, they all worked quietly, and a little awkwardly because of Nomi, on the next issue of the official paper, saving space for a story about the *Renegade Telegraph* and the school's reaction to it. Jamie kept worrying about Matt, who didn't return, and she expected to be called in herself before five o'clock, which was when Mr. Bartholomew usually left the building; he'd know, certainly, that the newspaper staff often worked late.

But no call came, and the next morning things seemed normal enough. Jamie had a full schedule of classes and wasn't able to look for Matt, but at lunch Terry said he hadn't seen him. Then right before afternoon classes started, a student came up to Jamie and said Mr. Bartholomew wanted to see her in his office.

Mr. Bartholomew was a heavy-set, graying man with a kind face; he was known both for his fairness and for his adherence to school rules. It didn't take him long to get to the point.

"Sit down, Jamie," he said, and when she'd settled herself in the large leather armchair opposite his desk, he asked, "You've been working on the *Telegraph* since you were a freshman, haven't you?"

"Yes."

"And I believe that you want to do newspaper work when

you're finished with your education, and that you're planning to major in journalism in college?"

"That's right," Jamie answered cautiously.

Mr. Bartholomew folded his hands and leaned back in his chair. "The *Telegraph*'s been good this year, Jamie, and it showed a marked improvement during the last couple of years as you emerged as its most dedicated reporter. You toed a dangerous line with your condom editorial, but I was proud of you, and I was sorry when Mrs. Buel and the school committee made such a fuss about it. I disagreed with the school committee's ruling—an editorial *is* opinion, certainly—but I did wish you'd gotten an op-ed for that issue."

"So did I. I tried, and maybe I should've tried harder. But . . ."

"That's done with now. I can understand the temptation you faced, the impulse you felt to put out a counter paper." He leaned forward. "In the real world, Jamie, that would be fine. But a high school isn't the real world, even though we try very hard to make it resemble the real world as much as possible. The fact remains that you should have gotten permission to distribute that paper, first from Matt and then from me."

"But—well—would you have given it?"

"I honestly don't know," Mr. Bartholomew admitted. "I would have wanted to. But Mrs. Buel is very much a presence these days, and I'm not willing to give her an opportunity to—let's just say I'm not willing to give her an opportunity. You can go on publishing your renegade paper, Jamie, with my unofficial blessing. But you cannot distribute it on school grounds or work on it on school time. You'll have to figure out another way to get it to the students, but I strongly suggest you avoid handing it out at the edge of school property, because even though that would fall within the letter of the law, Mrs. Buel would probably find some way to create a public uproar about it."

"But if I distributed it, say, on the town green or in Lang's Store or a couple of blocks away from school . . ."

"That would be fine. I don't think Mrs. Buel would be too happy about it, but she wouldn't have a legitimate complaint. After all, she could do the same thing, if she had a journalistic bent."

"Thank you," Jamie said contritely, both relieved and embarrassed. "And I really am sorry, Mr. Bartholomew. I didn't think about distribution. I didn't even know about the rule."

"Did you ever hear that ridiculous thing about ignorance of the law not being any excuse?"

Jamie nodded.

"I've never thought it was very fair. But lots of things aren't fair." He stood up and held out his hand. "You're a fine student, Jamie Crawford. And I expect Wilson High's going to number you among its highest-achieving students when you're out in that tough real world. Keep up the good work, but for heaven's sake, be careful!"

Jamie shook his offered hand. "I will." She turned to go and then turned back. "Mr. Bartholomew," she asked. "Is Mrs. Buel trying to control the school committee?"

"I don't know. It's the opinion of some of the faculty that she is. She certainly seems to want to impose her strong opinions on others. And she appears to have backing from some very powerful groups from out of state. There are people on the school committee who share her opinions. But they weren't very vocal till she came along. We live in a democracy,

Jamie. Mrs. Buel is entitled to her opinion, as you well know, just as you're entitled to yours. Good luck."

"Thank you, Mr. Bartholomew," Jamie said, and left.

She had one class with Terry that afternoon, and right before it she was able to tell him what Mr. Bartholomew had said. But she didn't see the others, so as soon as the last bell rang, she ran down the hall to the newspaper office, burst inside full of the good news that Mr. Bartholomew seemed to be on their side—and stopped. Terry was sitting silently at Matt's desk, Nomi had her hands over her face and her elbows on her drafting table, Tessa was shaking her head as if she'd heard something she couldn't believe, Jack was drumming a pencil on Jamie's desk, and Cindy, a folder of new ads still in her hand, was staring out the window.

Terry stood up when Jamie came in.

"It's Matt," he said. "The school committee's kicked him off the paper."

TWELVE

"What we heard wasn't official," Terry explained. "But, Cindy, you tell her."

"I had to find Matt to show him a new ad," Cindy said. "But I couldn't find him here or in his classroom, so I knocked on the teachers' room door and Mr. Gordon told me Matt had gone home and that he can go on teaching but he's been suspended from being our adviser. Something about being a disruptive influence or something."

Jamie threw herself into her desk chair. Tessa went over to her and put her hands on her shoulders for a moment, then sat down again. "It wasn't Matt's fault," Jamie said miserably. "Why didn't they suspend me? I just saw Mr. Bartholomew early this afternoon! How come he didn't tell me about Matt?"

Terry shrugged. "He probably didn't know yet. The school committee probably just told him. I think they had a special meeting at lunchtime."

"I don't see how they can do that legally," Jack said. "I mean, Matt didn't have anything to do with the *Renegade*."

"Yeah," said Terry. "But I think they're out to get him, and this gave them an opportunity."

"I still don't think it's legal," Jack said. "I hope he sues them."

"What are we supposed to do without him?" Nomi asked softly. "That's what I'd like to know."

"Complain," Terry said angrily. "Protest."

"Maybe," Jamie said thoughtfully. "I'd sure like to. But at least they didn't suspend him from teaching. Protesting might make things worse at this point. The school committee might be even surer then that he'd helped with the *Renegade*."

Jack sighed. "Jamie's right, guys," he said, and Nomi and Cindy both nodded slowly.

"Can't we at least complain?" Tessa asked angrily. "I mean it's horrible—unfair!"

Everyone looked at Jamie.

"The first thing we should do," she said, hoping she was right, "is go on with the *Telegraph*. Matt would want us to, I'm pretty sure. Besides," she added briskly, "I think Mr. Bartholomew's on our side." She explained about her talk with him; Cindy and Tessa looked pleased, but Nomi turned away. "So," she finished, "we just have to hand the *Renegade* out someplace else. And I don't see why we can't complain about the suspension, Tess, in the *Renegade*, and make it clear that Matt didn't have anything to do with our starting it. But meanwhile, we've got the regular paper to get out." She reached up to her "in" box, where reporters left their stories.

Before she could thumb through them, though, the door opened and Mr. Bartholomew appeared with the small dark woman, new that year, who taught freshman English; Jamie had seen her now and then in the halls. Shoulder-length, somewhat stringy hair swung on either side of her neck as she stood apologetically next to the principal.

"Jamie," said Mr. Bartholomew, looking more than a little uncomfortable. "Tessa—Terry—Cindy—Jack—Nomi. I—er— I have some—difficult news. I just got a call from the school committee about an hour ago, and they have—decided that Mr. Caggin should take some time off from his newspaper duties. He'll continue to teach, but I must ask you not to bother him with newspaper business for the time being." He cleared his throat, then awkwardly put his hand on the shoulder of the woman next to him. "Ms. Hinchley, here, has kindly agreed to take his place as newspaper adviser for a while. I'm sure you'll give her your utmost cooperation." Mr. Bartholomew let go of Ms. Hinchley's shoulder and started talking very fast, as if anxious to get what he had to say over with. "I've told Ms. Hinchley what a good group you are, and she already knows what a fine paper the *Telegraph* is. I know you'll all get along well and keep the paper going till Matt comes back. I know it's—er—a bit of an adjustment, but I also know you're equal to it." He put his hand on the doorknob, pausing momentarily; it's as if, Jamie thought, he wants to say a lot more than he's saying but doesn't think he can. "Well—carry on. Good luck. Let me know if I can be of any help. I'm sure you won't need it, though."

And before Jamie or anyone else could reply or ask questions, he left.

There was a heavy, stunned silence, while Ms. Hinchley looked nervously at each of them in turn.

Finally Tessa poked Jamie and said, "I'm Tessa Gillespie, photo editor. Which mostly means photographer, although a couple of other kids take pictures, too." She poked Jamie again.

"Jamie Crawford, editor in chief," Jamie said, and introduced Nomi, Terry, Jack, and Cindy.

Ms. Hinchley smiled tentatively. "Hi, all of you. I—um—I teach freshman English. Well, I guess you probably know that. And I know you're juniors and seniors. Mr. Bartholomew told me you're very—er—skillful journalists." Ms. Hinchley edged over to Matt's desk and sat down tentatively on his chair, as if she wasn't quite sure she belonged there. "I used to teach junior high in Georgeport, and we did a school paper there, so I guess that's why the school committee and Mr. Bartholomew asked me to, you know, fill in. I like your paper," she added shyly after a moment's silence. "It has wonderful possibilities, I think. You've got some very good writers, and . . ."

"Which paper?" Terry asked, his hostility barely concealed.

"Why, I meant—I mean—the Wilson High *Telegraph*, of course. I think we can all forget about that other paper, can't we? I mean, everyone can make mistakes. The job of a school paper," Ms. Hinchley said, sounding to Jamie as if she was parroting a textbook she'd read, "is to reflect the school community. It's really not supposed to be an investigative sheet or to dwell on controversy. Controversy," she went on, with increasing authority in her voice, "is divisive, and a good school paper is a unifying factor. Let's see what the *Telegraph* can do to bolster school spirit and bring the school community together."

"I didn't know it was apart," Terry muttered to Jamie.

Nomi, Jamie noticed, had looked pleased at what Ms. Hinchley had said about school spirit and the community, and was smiling, but Tessa and Cindy looked dismayed. Jack had gotten up and was pacing, as if he wanted to leave.

"Now," Ms. Hinchley said briskly, "what have we got for the next issue?"

"I don't believe her," Terry said, when they'd all left the office at the end of the day; they were clustered around Terry's car. "It's like she wants the paper to have about as much character as—as—oh, I don't know."

"Rice pudding," said Jamie. "Or a memo from the office. Rah, rah, Wilson, aren't we all wonderful and don't we all love each other. How many 'Blue Ribbon' features did she tell us to do?"

"Let's see." Jack counted them off on his fingers: "Student, Athlete, Teacher. Three so far."

"Oh, come on," Nomi said angrily. "That's not so bad. She's right that the paper's been too negative this year. You know how people always grumble about there being no good news in newspapers and on TV? Well, we were going in that direction. People don't just want to hear bad things."

"No," said Tessa, "but when there are bad things, people need to know about them."

"Not when they besmirch the name of good old Wilson High," Terry said sarcastically. "Give me a break!"

"Give us all a break," said Jamie. "I almost wouldn't mind quitting."

"Neither would I," said Cindy.

"Like little kids who can't have what they want?" Nomi said. "Or sore losers? I thought you were both better than that!"

"Whoa, Nomi!" Terry said, as Jamie, hurt, tried to think of a reply. "Haven't you ever heard of social protest? I think it's a great idea. We could close down the *Telegraph*, at least till they let Matt come back, and . . ."

". . . and put out the *Renegade Telegraph* instead," Tessa finished. "Sometimes you're almost a genius, Terry, you know?"

Nomi's eyes clouded; Jamie took a step toward her, then pulled back as Jack shouted gleefully, "A newspaper strike!"

Jamie considered that for a moment, then discarded it. "I guess a strike would be a good way to protest Matt's suspension or leave or whatever they're going to call it," she said slowly. "But I'd still be worried it might make things worse. And shouldn't we try to save what we can of the old *Telegraph*? Don't we owe that to Matt?"

"Yeah," said Terry, but he sounded deflated nonetheless. "You're right. Again."

"You are," Jack agreed.

"I guess," Tessa said, and Cindy nodded slowly, saying, "Okay."

"Nomi?" Jamie asked, trying to sound neutral. "Can you accept that? Can you work with us on the *Telegraph*?"

Nomi hesitated. "I'll try," she said at last. "I can probably work with Ms. Hinchley, anyway."

Tessa shifted her camera bag's position on her shoulder. "So okay. Nomi stays with the *Telegraph*, and the rest of us do both papers, at least for a while. Right?"

"Right," Jamie said. "Thank you, Nomi," she called as Nomi walked away. Nomi gave a tentative wave and went on walking.

Terry unlocked his car. "Okay. It's decided, then. Hey, I've got to go. Want a ride, anyone?"

"Sure," Cindy said. "Come on, Jack."

Jamie glanced at Tessa, who shook her head. "No thanks, Terry," Jamie said.

Tessa startled Jamie by draping her arm casually across Jamie's shoulders; Jamie tried unsuccessfully to ignore it. "She needs to calm down," Tessa said to Terry. "I've got to walk her, you know, like a crying baby. She looks calm, but I can tell she's going to explode if she doesn't move."

Terry held up one hand, palm out. "Peace," he said, going around to the driver's side as Jack maneuvered Cindy around to the passenger side. "Let me know when you want to start work on the next issue of the *Renegade*."

"Soon," Jamie shouted as he got in and slammed his door. "We can talk at lunch tomorrow. Bring ideas."

Terry beeped his horn and Tessa removed her arm from Jamie's shoulder, waving as he drove off.

Tessa turned to Jamie. "You're really boiling about that suspension, aren't you?"

"Yeah," Jamie said. "Yeah, I'm really boiling. But I'm also really excited, because I think we can do some good with the *Renegade*. We're free, Tess, with that paper, at least! Freedom of the press, like it says in the Constitution."

"First Amendment to the Constitution," Tessa corrected. "Did anyone ever tell you that you look—um—very mad when you're mad?"

The next day, when Jamie walked into health class, which had continued despite the absence of the textbook, Ms. Frick, the teacher, was late. By the time she arrived, the classroom was buzzing and Brandon Tomkins and Al Checkers were having what they called a scientific paper-airplane contest near the window. Jamie was glad to see that Terry and Ernie, sitting near the back, seemed deep in conversation.

Ms. Frick came in so quietly Jamie didn't even see her till she heard her say, "Class."

The strain in her voice, which was usually calm, made Jamie look up. The room fell silent, and Brandon and Al quickly pocketed their planes.

"Class, I have some bad news." Ms. Frick sat on the edge of her desk, as she often did. "Or maybe it'll be good news to some of you; I'm not sure. For at least the next few weeks, you'll all have a study this period. Health class has been indefinitely suspended while the school committee and a special committee of—er—parents study the curriculum."

There were a couple of quiet cheers, followed by a good deal of loud murmuring, and Jamie felt herself go cold inside.

"So," Ms. Frick said, "that's it, unless there are any questions?"

Jamie raised her hand. "Was this the school committee's decision?" she asked. "Or Mr. Bartholomew's, or whose?"

"As I understand it," Ms. Frick said, "that new group, Families for Traditional Values, got copies of the health education curriculum for all the town's schools, after the school committee impounded the textbooks and temporarily suspended condom distribution. They studied the curriculum and the books, and then went to the school committee with a list of complaints. They sent a petition around . . ."

"Yeah," said Al Checkers. "My folks signed it."

"So did mine," said Ernie.

"Mine didn't," Jamie said. "They didn't even get it, as far as I know."

Terry and several others said theirs hadn't gotten it either.

"Interesting," Ms. Frick commented. "Just out of curiosity, how many of you know your parents got the petition?"

About a third of the class raised their hands.

Terry snickered. "Looks like FTV did a pretty selective poll."

"I don't know about that," said Ms. Frick, "but I guess they collected enough signatures to get the school committee to reconsider."

"What are they planning to do?" asked Vicky Chase, in the next row over from Jamie.

"I'm not sure. I think they want to rewrite the health curriculum, or parts of it anyway."

"The sex parts," said Terry.

Al said, "You got that right," under his breath. At the same time, Brandon guffawed, and then clapped his hand over his mouth and widened his eyes as if pretending to be shocked.

"Yes," said Ms. Frick, glaring at them. "I'm sorry. In fact, I'm very sorry. If any of you have questions or want to talk about anything related to the old curriculum, please feel free to come to me."

Silence followed her invitation. "Okay, then," Ms. Frick went on. "I guess you should all get started on some homework."

"It's true," Jamie's mother said when Jamie and Tessa burst into the Crawfords' kitchen after school; at lunch, they had decided, along with Terry, Jack, and Cindy, to devote the next issue of the *Renegade* to both suspensions, Matt's and the health curriculum's. "We got the same edict at the middle school," Mrs. Crawford told Jamie and Tessa, "and so did the elementary school. Lisa Buel strikes again."

"I don't get it," Jamie fumed. "I don't get how she can have so much power."

"She's got people behind her now, Jamie; she's been talking—campaigning, almost. A lot of people at Lord's Assembly are on her side, but she's convinced many others as well. She's also got support from that organization that printed the pamphlet you showed Dad and me." Mrs. Crawford sat down at the kitchen table. "And since sex education's an explosive issue all over the country . . ."

"Yes!" Jamie exclaimed excitedly. "There's the focus!"

Tessa raised her eyebrows and sat down next to Mrs. Crawford. "Has she always been like this?"

"Always." Mrs. Crawford looked amused. "You just have to wait till she decides to fill the rest of us in."

Jamie leaned against the sink. "The health curriculum piece," she said, after explaining briefly to her mother about the *Renegade*'s next issue. "We could do a real in-depth piece on sex education. I was already thinking of interviewing Mrs. Buel and maybe Ms. Frick, but we could expand it—not just the controversy about sex ed in Wilson, but the controversy in Wilson compared to the controversy in other towns. I could hunt up some information on what you were saying, Mom, about problems all over the country. There's got to be some stuff in the library."

"There is," Mrs. Crawford told her. "Quite a lot, in fact. We got the town library to order some books for us last summer when we were working on the health curriculum. And then we suggested a few additions to the school library, once we settled on it. But the town library's your best bet, I think. There are lots of newspaper articles there, too, *The New York Times* and *The Boston Globe* and the Georgeport paper. But, Jamie, are you sure this is a good idea? Doing all this in the *Renegade*?"

"You bet I do. I think it's *necessary* to do it. I'm pretty sure

Ms. Hinchley isn't going to let us even mention Matt's suspension or the health ed curriculum in the *Telegraph*. The kids have a right to know what's going on."

"Oh, Jamie," said her mother softly. "I love the fire in you. But I don't want you to get hurt, or suspended yourself."

"It's in a good cause," Jamie said fiercely.

"Yes," said Mrs. Crawford, "it is."

Jamie looked at the kitchen clock. "Library's still open. How about it, Tess?"

"Sure." Tessa stood.

"Supper," Mrs. Crawford called, "is at six-thirty, Jamie. Pick me up some milk at Lang's Store on your way back? I was so steamed up myself about the health ed curriculum I forgot."

The Wilson Public Library, it turned out, kept back issues of *The New York Times* and *The Boston Globe*, plus a few other papers, for only two years, in a special room in the basement. "For anything more than two years old," the reference librarian told them, "you'll have to go to Georgeport and read the papers on microfilm."

"That's okay," Jamie replied. "Two years back ought to be enough anyway. Thanks."

"Why don't I look for books," Tessa suggested as Jamie headed for the stairs to the basement, "while you check out the papers? Then I'll come help you."

"Okay."

A few minutes later, Jamie was in a damp and dimly lit basement room, scribbling notes from articles listed under sex education in *The New York Times Index*. She'd gotten through about a month's worth when Tessa returned.

"What've you got?" Jamie asked, stretching and then rubbing her cramped right hand.

Tessa sat down beside her. "Nothing. Absolutely nothing."

"Huh? But Mom said . . ."

"I know. And there are books listed in the computer catalogue. But they're out. I decided to check the shelves anyway, just to make sure; that's what took me so long, that and asking the librarian, who was waiting on someone. When she was finally free, she said she was really sorry but she couldn't tell me who has the books, just that they've been checked out. She said she could put a reserve on them, but that probably won't do us any good; they're not due for another couple of weeks. Someone else beat us to it." Tessa picked up one of the newspapers. "How're you doing with this?"

"Great. We probably don't need the books anyway. There's a lot here. Want to help?"

"Sure."

Jamie gestured to the shelves. "Why don't you take the *Globe*? We can split up the other New England papers, probably."

"Okay."

By the time they left the library, they each had several pages of notes, and Jamie felt confident that she had enough material to write a really good feature. And after dinner that night, Jamie called Lisa Buel to ask her for an interview.

"No, dear," Mrs. Buel said. "Thank you for the opportunity. But I really don't have anything to say right now. We're studying the curriculums, and when we're through, we'll make recommendations to the school committee."

"Is 'we' Families for Traditional Values?" asked Jamie.

"Yes, it is."

"I get the feeling," said Jamie, "that your group is against sex education in general. Is that true?"

"I told you," said Mrs. Buel smoothly but with an angry edge to her voice, "that I don't have anything to say right now."

"May I call you again when you've made some kind of decision?"

"You certainly are a very persistent young lady. Yes, I suppose you can call me."

"Thank you."

Jamie hung up and dialed Morris Just.

"I'm not sure what's going on," Mr. Just said. "But yes, that FTV group, through Mrs. Buel, is looking at the health curriculum at all levels. I guess that's their right; it's any citizen's right. A couple of school committee members are also in FTV, which makes the situation a bit more complicated."

"Do you think the curriculum needs looking at?"

"No," said Mr. Just. "I don't. The school committee passed on the health curriculum when it was adopted late last summer, before Mrs. Buel was elected. And it has faculty and administrative support at all three of the town's schools, elementary, middle, and secondary."

"What does FTV have against it?"

"You were at that meeting, Jamie. If you want to know more, you'd better ask them. I don't want to lose my temper."

Jamie laughed. "Okay. Thanks, Mr. Just."

THIRTEEN

The next day, Jamie could barely keep her eyes open. She'd been up most of the night writing an editorial for the Wilson High *Telegraph*, plus her sex education article for the *Renegade Telegraph*, and was still polishing both at lunch. Terry looked miserable, but before Jamie had a chance to talk with him, Jack and Cindy, who had volunteered to write about Matt's suspension, handed her a draft of their piece. "We talked to him off the record," Jack told her, "on background, so we can't quote him. But we did find out stuff about his qualifications and we've used that."

"Off the record Matt said he's proud of us," Cindy added. "And he said he'll back us if we get into trouble, but he's pretty sure the school committee won't listen to him."

"Some of them won't, I bet," Jamie said. "And we sure don't want to get him fired. When can he come back to the paper?"

"I don't know," Jack told her. "He didn't say."

"He said he's glad his wife works," Cindy said, "in case they do fire him. That was an attempt at a joke, I think, but we got the feeling he's more upset than he let on. Right, Jack?"

Jack nodded. "He's hurt, too, we're pretty sure."

"Anyway," Cindy said, "someone want to read the piece over? Please?"

"I think it's a little rough here," Jack said. He took the draft back and pointed to a paragraph in the middle. "I'm not sure about this transition."

Terry and Jamie both held out their hands.

"Here. I'll do it," Terry said. "You've got other stuff to do, Jamie. I'll give it to you when it looks ready."

"Okay," Jamie said dubiously; Terry's voice sounded strained and he looked miserable. "But . . ."

"Later." Terry got up from the table.

"Right," Jamie said, even more dubiously. "Later." She returned to her *Telegraph* editorial.

Jamie had no chance that afternoon to talk with Terry privately, except briefly about the Matt piece, which had turned out to need very little work except for the one transition Jack had pointed out. Then, after school in the newspaper office, Ms. Hinchley read Jamie's editorial and quickly handed it back to her. "Sorry," she said. "But I think you know why we can't run this."

"No," Jamie said, bristling, while Tessa and Nomi looked up from the layout table, where they were arranging photos, and Terry put his pencil down from marking up an article about the most recent football victory. "No, I don't know. Why not?"

"We were told that editorials should reflect both sides of whatever issue they're about. This doesn't. And I think you know that perfectly well."

"I've mentioned both points of view. And I . . ."

Tessa got up and stood behind Jamie. "Easy," she said quietly.

"If you want to rewrite it, fine," Ms. Hinchley said with

more force than Jamie expected of her. "If not, either write another or we'll do without."

"I'll write another," Jamie snapped, plunking her first one down on her desk and yanking her computer keyboard toward her. Tessa returned to the layout table as Jamie's fingers pounded on the keys.

"Smoking computer," Jamie heard Terry say, and she was dimly aware of Tessa's answering chuckle, but only dimly; her mind was on her words:

Editorial
THE NEW *TELEGRAPH*

With this issue, folks, we launch a new kind of newspaper. Despite recent upheavals—the suspension of Matt Caggin as this paper's faculty adviser and the recent suspension of health classes while Families for Traditional Values studies the textbooks and the curriculum—the *Telegraph*, under its new faculty adviser, Ms. Dawn Hinchley, will concentrate on pulling the school together, and on GOOD news, not bad. It is the job of a school paper, Ms. Hinchley tells us, to foster unity and school spirit, and so from now on, that will be our mission. We hope you'll be cheered by each and every issue!

"Change 'despite' to 'because of,' " Ms. Hinchley said when Jamie had handed it to her, "and we'll run it."

"And if I don't?" asked Jamie.

"And if you don't, we won't run it."

"Change it," Terry advised her. "The kids'll get it," he added under his breath.

Jamie highlighted "Despite," banged "Because of" in its

place, and slammed out of the office, just barely managing to snarl, "Back in a minute," as she left. She headed straight for the girls' room, where she leaned against one of the sinks, still fuming.

"Cold water," said Tessa, coming in and turning on a faucet, "does wonders."

Jamie splashed her face. "I could kill her!" she shouted. "I could just kill her. She's not a newspaper person, she's a— Oh, I don't know what she is."

"She's doing what she was told to do," Tessa said calmly. "I think the school's scared. I think Mr. Bartholomew and whoever else is in charge is scared of Mrs. Buel and FTV, and they're going to do anything they can to keep her from attacking them or really harming them. You read the same stuff I did, Jamie; you know people can be really vicious about sex education. I don't think anyone wants that to happen here."

"Well, I don't either," Jamie barked. "But I also don't want us to give in. The school committee voted on that curriculum and on making condoms available, too, although everyone seems to have forgotten about that. How can one woman overthrow a vote?"

"By getting enough support for there to be another vote. You know that. Hey, that's the American way."

"Yeah, I know." Jamie leaned against one of the sinks. "And if it were me trying to get something changed, I'd do everything I could to be successful at it, too. Maybe I'll write about that next time." Then to her horror, Jamie burst into tears.

Instantly, Tessa was beside her, holding her. "Hey," she crooned softly, rubbing Jamie's back. "Hey. You can say anything you want in the *Renegade*; you know that." She tipped

Jamie's head up and, taking a tissue out of her pocket, dried Jamie's eyes. "Like your mom, I like the fire in you. You're quite a person, my friend, you know that?"

There was a click; the door to the girls' room opened, and Jamie, feeling instantly guilty, sprang away from Tessa; Tessa looked surprised and, Jamie realized, not at all guilty. Why should she, she thought bitterly. I'm the only one who's got feelings to hide.

Karen Hodges stood in the doorway, staring.

"I left my jacket somewhere," she said after a moment. "I— Well, it doesn't look like it's in here."

"No," Jamie said shakily. "I haven't seen it."

"Me neither," Tessa said, watching Jamie, an odd expression on her face. She put her hand on Jamie's arm. "You feeling okay now?" she asked loudly, as if for Karen's benefit.

Jamie nodded.

"Oh?" said Karen, sounding surprised, then skeptical. "Was that it? I thought . . ."

"Never you mind what you thought." Tessa herded her out. "You just keep your thoughts to yourself. And I hope you find your jacket," she called after her.

When Karen was gone, Tessa faced Jamie. "Jamie," she asked gently, "am I crazy or is there something going on here that I should know about? You jumped away from me like you'd been shot. Or like . . . Well, sort of like you felt guilty."

Jamie turned away. "No. No, nothing's going on," she lied miserably.

Tessa shrugged and moved to the door. But then she turned and, in a very quiet, firm voice, said, "Jamie, I'm your friend. And when I'm friends with someone, that's all that counts with me, okay?"

The words TELL HER thundered in Jamie's mind. But all she actually said, in a voice she struggled to keep steady, was "Thanks, Tessa. That's what counts with me, too."

That night, Jamie called Terry. "Okay, come on. Tell me. Something's happened, right?"

"Yeah. Right." Terry's voice sounded unnaturally cheerful. "Well, I saw it coming, you know? I wasn't surprised."

"You saw what coming?"

"Ernie. He's decided he's straight. Or he wants to be, anyway. He's going to stay with Vicky. He says she's wonderful, very patient and understanding, blah, blah, blah. They're—I don't know—having a big-deal relationship or something. As if Vicky could ever stick to one person."

"Oh, Terry!"

"Yeah, well, like I said, I knew. Pretty much. And I don't want to talk about it, okay? I was so shook about it, Mom asked what was wrong, and I fell apart telling her. I'll bawl again if you're nice to me, Jamie, so please, just let me get used to it for a while. Okay?"

"Okay," she said, aching for him. "But I'm here if you need me, Terry, okay?"

"Sure. Thanks. Goodbye."

On Monday morning, Jamie, Tessa, Terry, and Jack—Cindy had to study for a test—each took a corner two streets away from school and passed out copies of the *Renegade Telegraph* as people arrived. This issue was both sides of two pages, stapled together. Cindy and Jack's piece about Matt's suspension, with a photo by Tessa, was on the first page, running over onto the second, where there was also a brief editorial, and Jamie and Tessa's sex education feature was on the third and fourth. Copies of the Wilson High *Telegraph* were, as usual, in bins by the school's front door, but almost everyone, including the faculty, had read the *Renegade* before they'd even picked up the *Telegraph*.

This time, though, there was sudden laughter as Jamie walked past where Brandon, Al, and Sam Mills were standing with a few other boys near the front door. "Ooooh," she heard Sam say in falsetto as he dangled a copy of the *Renegade* delicately between his thumb and forefinger. "This is *such* a sexy paper!"

"Those who can't do it write about it," Brandon said loudly as Jamie went by. "Know what I mean, butch?"

"Sweet seventeen," someone else called out, "and never been kissed—not *normally*, anyway."

Ignore them, Jamie said to herself as she walked on. *Don't listen. They're just bored.*

But when she saw that Karen Hodges was standing with the boys, her whole body suddenly felt chilled.

It wasn't very far into the day before Jamie was called into Mr. Bartholomew's office, along with Tessa, Terry, Jack, and Cindy. Ms. Hinchley was already there when they arrived.

"Sit down," Mr. Bartholomew said; Jamie could see copies of both papers on his desk. "You've had a busy week," he said dryly, leaning back and lacing his hands together. "I know you're angry and upset at losing Mr. Caggin as your adviser. And apparently you're angry about the health class suspension, although I don't think that feeling is shared by your classmates, most of whom are just as happy to have an extra study period and less homework. You've followed the letter of my ruling by passing out your renegade paper a little away from school property, although I'd be more comfortable if you'd done it farther away. And you've cooperated, on the surface anyway, with Ms. Hinchley, after, shall we say, a rocky start. But Ms. Hinchley has, rightly, pointed out some concerns that I think are legitimate. Ms. Hinchley?"

Ms. Hinchley's mouth was tight and her words were clipped as she spoke. "I think it's obvious," she said, "that you're subverting the *Telegraph*. The legitimate *Telegraph*. And I'm sure you're well aware of that. In fact, I think that's your goal."

"Our goal is to get the news out to the students," Jamie replied, trying to sound as pleasant and reasonable as she could. "Since it looks as if we can't do that in the regular paper, we're doing it on our own. I don't see that we've broken any rules."

"You haven't," Ms. Hinchley said crisply. "But you've created a conflict of interest for yourselves, and you're spreading yourselves very thin. I don't see how you can possibly have the commitment the Wilson High *Telegraph* needs as long as you're publishing your own paper at the same time. You're going to wear yourselves out, and your schoolwork is bound to suffer. It's hard enough doing one paper; two should be just about impossible, even if the second one doesn't come out as often. I think, and Mr. Bartholomew agrees with me, that if you're going to publish the *Renegade* regularly, you may soon find you'll need to choose between it and the *Telegraph*— which will go on publishing," she added, "regardless of your decision."

Jamie glanced at the others; Terry and Tessa nodded imperceptibly, Cindy and Jack more obviously. "I think I can manage both," Jamie said. "I don't like choosing, but if I have to, I'll choose the *Renegade*."

"So will I," Cindy said.

Jack nodded. "Me, too."

Tessa and Terry nodded.

"Okay," said Mr. Bartholomew. "So be it. But—and this goes for each of you—if your grades suffer because you're working on two papers, we'll have to ask you to drop one. If you won't drop the *Renegade*, we'll have to require that you drop the *Telegraph*. Understood?"

"Understood," Jamie said, and the others nodded again.

"One more thing," Mr. Bartholomew added. "I admire you for your idealism and the depth of your commitment, but please be careful. I trust that your good journalistic sense will keep you from libeling anyone. Just remember that what you're doing with the *Renegade* is in no way connected to the school, and that the school won't be able to support you if it backfires. Are you aware of that?"

They all nodded once more.

"Very well," said Mr. Bartholomew. "Thank you for your time. And remember what I said about your grades. It would be very unwise to let them slip."

"Well, looks like we're on," Terry said as he and Jamie followed Jack, Cindy, and Tessa out of Mr. Bartholomew's office. The hall was empty except for some students putting up posters about a costume party to be held at Cindy's that Saturday, which was Halloween. "I offer my room as the *Renegade*'s new home. I have lots of time. Time, space, and dedication," he said bitterly. "No distractions, except the *Tele-*

graph. It's great not to have a social life. A—whatever. I'm yours, *Renegade* editor, all yours."

"He'll be back," Jamie said softly.

"Oh, please," Terry said. "What are you, Madame Crawford, Seer?"

"Maybe," Jamie said, putting on an accent and seizing Terry's hand as if about to read his palm.

But Terry shook her hand off.

FOURTEEN

"Terry's gay, isn't he?" Tessa asked without preamble the next afternoon at Jamie's house. "I don't have a date for Cindy's party," she had told Jamie earlier, "and if you don't either, why don't we go together?" Jamie had agreed, although a little nervously, and invited Tessa over to decide on costumes.

"It's okay," Tessa said now, before Jamie could answer. "I won't say anything to anyone. But I heard Brandon and Al talking and Sam and Karen and some other kids, too, and— Well, it's kind of obvious Terry's upset about Ernie and Vicky. Brandon sure seems to have a gay thing, the way he calls you butch all the time." She looked closely at Jamie. "You're upset about it, too, aren't you?"

"Yes," Jamie said. She hesitated, then decided to assume Tessa meant Ernie and Vicky by "it," even though she knew that wasn't necessarily true. "Let's just say I don't like to see Terry hurt. And he is hurt now, very."

"If I were gay," Tessa said, looking out Jamie's window, "I don't think I'd hide it. Or I'd hide it completely, never give anyone a clue."

Jamie couldn't think of anything to say.

There was a very long pause.

"So," said Tessa, turning to face Jamie again, "what shall we go as?"

"Editor and photographer?" Jamie suggested weakly. "But I guess that would be kind of obvious."

"Mickey and Minnie Mouse?" Tessa said, then clapped her hand to her head dramatically. "No, bad idea! Brandon would love it." She looked closely at Jamie, then sat down on Jamie's bed. "Sorry! How about—how about bears? A couple of sexless bears?"

"Sexless bears?"

"Yeah. Sexless bears. We dress in old brown rugs or something, so no one can tell who we are. Or what sex we are. Or anything."

"I like it. Of course Terry's going as a vampire, but . . ."

"So we won't win the horror prize. Who cares? At least we'll be warm if it's a cold night."

It was a cold night, with a bone-chilling wind off the water; Jamie was glad for the warmth of her bear costume. It wasn't exactly an old rug; she and Tessa had found some brown bath towels in a discount store in Georgeport and had fashioned their bear suits out of them. They'd even found bear masks, and had glued some of the toweling to them in the appropriate places.

The lawn in front of Cindy's house was festooned with lighted jack-o'-lanterns and ghostly sheet-clad lampposts. Several costumed children carrying paper trick-or-treat bags and flashlights passed as Jamie and Tessa arrived in Tessa's mother's car, with Tessa's camera stashed under the front seat. Just as they parked, a skeleton drove up, hopped out of his car, and opened the passenger door for a gypsy.

"That's Ernie and Vicky," Jamie said, recognizing them just before the skeleton settled a skull mask over his head.

"Poor Terry," said Tessa, her voice muffled by her mask.

"Yes," Jamie answered as they went inside and were greeted by Jack, his flamboyant good looks accentuated by a splashy gangster outfit. "Poor Terry."

But Terry, arriving a little later in his vampire costume, gave Ernie only the most cursory of glances and strode right over to where Jamie and Tessa were sitting near the CD player.

"You are holdink ze how-you-say editorial meeteeng?" he asked in a fake all-purpose accent.

"Ooooh, a vampire!" Tessa shrieked, hand over her heart.

"Nein, mein Herr," said Jamie in a growly bear voice. "We're waiting for the third bear."

"The third bear." Terry sat down beside them, his eyes, Jamie could see, now following Ernie's every move. "But is there a third bear? Is there ever a third bear? If there is no third bear in sight, does a third bear exist? Excuse me." He got up and sidled toward the other side of the room as Ernie and Vicky sat down on a couch there.

Tessa whispered to Jamie, "Did you notice that he recognized us right away?"

"It could be because I told him we were going as bears."

Tessa batted Jamie with her paw. "Could be, yeah."

Someone in an astronaut suit turned off the CD player and popped a tape into the deck below it, and suddenly everyone was dancing. Nomi, in a long white-and-gold dress with a gold crown on her head and a gold scepter in her hand, danced by with Clark, who was dressed in a somewhat moth-eaten tux. A ghost in a flowing sheet floated toward Jamie and Tessa and, tweaking her mask aside just enough to reveal that she was Cindy, said, "Anyone covering this bash? It's a natural for Hinchley." She floated off again, this time into Jack-the-gangster's arms, without waiting for an answer. The doorbell rang, and the astronaut answered it, letting in two small children dressed as the Tin Man and the Scarecrow; the astronaut stuffed candy from a bowl near the door into their bags and drifted weightlessly back into the room. Two witches and a wizard, forming a triangle as they danced, crowded against Jamie's knees as the music grew more frantic, and Tessa, grabbing Jamie's paw, growled, "Come on!" pulling her to her feet. In a moment they were dancing, too, clumsy in their bear suits, whirling and bobbing to the music, and even though Jamie was nervous about it, no one seemed to notice or care that they were both girls. After all, the witches were girls, too, although of course they were also dancing with the wizard—and, Jamie told herself, straight girls do dance together sometimes. Besides, maybe on Halloween such things don't matter; maybe on Halloween anything is possible.

Someone tugged at her furry arm, and she turned to see Karen Hodges, thinly disguised as Heidi, looking up at her. "You're Jamie Crawford," Karen said, her brown braids incongruous against her far-from-innocent face. "And you're dancing with *her*. Aren't you?"

Jamie gave a bear growl in response as Tessa danced in front of Karen, cutting her off from Jamie. "Little bitch," Tessa said into Jamie's ear. "What is *with* her?"—and then they were apart again, dancing with the others; Jamie was hot under her bear suit, but it was wonderful to be dancing with Tessa, wonderful to be with all of them, actually; all friends—except of course for Karen Hodges—all celebrating.

The music slowed and couples moved closer together;

Jamie saw the vampire look longingly at the skeleton, who seemed stiff and awkward as he held the gypsy, moving with her but aloof. The music slowed even more, and someone turned off a light or two—

And then the door flew open and someone yelled, "Fire!"

Jamie smelled smoke as she and Tessa hurried with the others to the door. When they were all outside, most masks off now, sniffing, looking anxiously at the roof, at the houses on either side and opposite, Tessa grabbed her camera out of the car and called to Jamie, "Look at the sky!" and Jamie saw a deep orange-red glow over the harbor.

"It's the yacht basin!" someone shouted.

"No, it's near Sloan's Beach. There's summer cottages there—maybe it's them. Come on!"

The costumed crowd surged toward the beach, stumbling through the dark streets in their unfamiliar clothes, tripping over long skirts and clunking in heavy boots. Jamie felt awkward in her bear suit; Tessa was faster, lither than she, and she thought incongruously how little she really knew her and how exciting it was to keep discovering new things, even if they never became more than friends.

And then they turned down the last street, tore through the parking lot, where there were, Jamie saw, several cars; they burst onto the beach . . .

And stopped.

Black silhouetted figures swarmed like demons around a blazing bonfire, feeding it logs and small oblong boards . . .

No.

Not boards at all, Jamie realized.

"Books!" Tessa's horrified whisper echoed Jamie's. "They're burning books!"

November

FIFTEEN

The Wilson News-Courier

FTV BURNS BOOKS
Halloween Bonfire Shocks Many

Halloween revelers from Wilson High were shocked last night to discover adults from the new group Families for Traditional Values (FTV) on Sloan's Beach, tossing books into a bonfire. "They were dancing around it like it was some kind of witches' sabbat," said Jamie Crawford, editor in chief of the school newspaper, the Wilson High *Telegraph*, who, with several of her friends (one of whom, Tessa Gillespie, took the photo that accompanies this article), discovered the blaze.

"It was necessary to do something dramatic in order to make our point," Lisa Buel, founder of FTV, told this reporter. "There are a number of highly inappropriate books in the town library, and several in the school libraries, most of them acquired when the new sex education curriculum was introduced. Children have free access to them; they need to be kept in a locked case, accessible only to adults . . ."

Jamie threw the town paper down in disgust. "Look at this!" she shouted. "Mrs. Buel comes right out and says they took those books out of the library in order to burn them! That's why they were checked out when Tessa and I looked for them! No one has the right to do that. No one."

"Slow down, Jamie!" Her father peered over her shoulder; it was nearly lunchtime on the day after the Halloween party. "Read on. It says here"—he pointed farther down the *News-Courier*'s page—"that they bought copies of the books to burn and that they're holding on to the library books."

"Oh, so that makes it all right?" Jamie said, still shouting. "They're just covering themselves by doing that. Burning books is wrong no matter whose they are."

"Jamie, Jamie." Her father put his hand on her shoulder. "Calm down. People can do what they want with their own property, and that includes books. Be fair."

Jamie slumped down in her chair. "Yeah, okay. But it's the principle of the thing."

"It sure is." Mrs. Crawford came into the room with Ronnie and peered over Jamie's shoulder.

"There's your story, then, Jamie." Her father opened the refrigerator and handed a half-gallon container of milk to Jamie and a package of lunch ham to Ronnie. "For I assume," he said, turning around and giving Jamie a long look, "that you're going to write about this in that renegade paper of yours. Is there any roast beef left over from last night?"

"Yes," said Mrs. Crawford. "Second shelf, on the left. Ronnie, please put the ham down before you drop it. Jamie, glasses, please. Where's the bread?"

"You bet I'm going to write about it," Jamie said, getting up for the glasses.

"What about lunch?" asked her mother.

"Not hungry." Jamie put three glasses on the table and left the kitchen.

"Great photo!" her father called after her. "Good for Tess!"

Jamie spent the next hour on the phone. Yes, the assistant town librarian could provide a list of the books, but she'd have to ask her supervisor for permission to release it; yes, the school librarian, when Jamie called her at home, said she'd checked out some books to an adult recently, but she couldn't say which ones or to whom; no, Lisa Buel wouldn't consent to be interviewed by Jamie; yes, Mom would try to find out what books were involved if the library couldn't give Jamie the titles; yes, Tessa, Terry, Cindy, and Jack would be right over.

"We both think what happened last night was awful," said Cindy, sitting next to Jack on Jamie's bed. "I mean, it *was* awful. No one has the right to burn library books."

"They didn't," Jamie said. "They bought other copies of the books and burned those. They still have the library books, but . . ."

"Why?" asked Jack, putting his arm around Cindy.

"Huh?"

"Why do they still have them?"

"Yeah," said Tessa. "It's like they're holding them hostage or something."

"Maybe they are," Jamie said thoughtfully. "Anyway, obviously we've got to cover the burning in the *Renegade*—fast. I wish we could get an interview with Lisa Buel."

"Yeah, right," Terry said sarcastically.

"Can't we?" Cindy asked.

Jamie shook her head. "She wouldn't talk to me before, and she won't now either. I tried."

"Maybe we could at least ask her to confirm what she told the town paper," Tessa suggested.

Jack nodded. "It couldn't hurt to try."

"Good idea. Okay," Jamie said briskly. "Let's get going so we can have papers tomorrow morning."

Late that afternoon, when Jamie was in her room trying to draft the *Renegade*'s lead article, her mother came in and silently put a sheet of paper on her desk. "These are the books Lisa Buel took out of both libraries," she told her. "They're the only ones she's taken out at all recently, so they've got to be the ones she burned."

"You really got the librarians to tell you?"

"Let's just say I found out."

Jamie grinned. "Okay," she said. "Wow, Mom! Thank you!" Then she scanned the list—and felt the same chill run through her as she had when Karen had come into the girls' room and when Brandon and the others called out their comments in the hall. Of the books on the list, most, fiction and nonfiction, dealt with homosexuality or AIDS, and several were about sex education in general.

"Damn her," Jamie said under her breath.

Mrs. Crawford pulled the spare chair up to Jamie's desk and sat down, watching Jamie carefully. "Are you still sure you want to be involved in this?"

"Yes, I want to be involved," Jamie said tensely. "I am involved," she added, thinking of the pamphlet as well as of FTV's choice of books. "I'm . . ."

"You're what?"

"Nothing," Jamie said gruffly. She'd been about to say *I guess I'm one of the people Lisa Buel's after,* but she felt herself shiver involuntarily as soon as she realized it.

I want to tell Mom, she thought. I want so much to tell her. But won't it hurt her? Terry's mother cried when he told her . . .

Maybe it would be selfish to tell her . . .

Jamie was still agonizing, searching unsuccessfully for tactful words, when her mother got up and put her hands on her shoulders. "I just want you to know," Mrs. Crawford said quietly, "that I think you're very brave and that I love you very much. And that I'm here if there's ever anything you want to talk to me about." She turned Jamie around and looked into her eyes. "Jamie, I don't shock easily. And I know God made all kinds of people. You should know that I understand that." She paused. "You do know that, don't you?"

Jamie felt her heart speed up; it was almost as if her mother knew already but wanted Jamie to say it. After all, Terry's father said he'd suspected about Terry, and he was okay about it. So why can't I say it, Jamie thought. Why can't I just say the words?

But she couldn't. Not yet, anyway.

Maybe because saying them would make it true.

But it was true.

Wasn't it?

It was true even if Lisa Buel was awful about it, true no matter how homophobic FTV was, or Brandon and Al and Sam and Karen and others were, true whether Tessa was straight or gay, true no matter what books were burned . . .

"Mom. Mom, I . . ." Jamie began after her mother had given her a quick kiss on the forehead and was moving quickly to the door.

Mrs. Crawford turned back. "Yes?"

But the moment had passed. "Nothing. Just—well, thanks, that's all."

Her mother smiled. "You're welcome," she said, "although I haven't done much yet."

You will, Jamie thought as her mother left. I'm pretty sure you will.

SIXTEEN

Early Monday morning, Jamie, Tessa, Cindy, Jack, and Terry again stationed themselves on corners a couple of streets away from school, each with a supply of *Renegade Telegraph*s to distribute.

By first period, nearly everyone at Wilson High had a copy of the latest issue, and most of them seemed to be reading the lead article about the book burning: the facts and a few quotes, including one Cindy and Jack had managed to get from Mrs. Buel saying that FTV planned to pay the fines for the books they still had and that they'd offered to buy the town library a locked case for them. The article ended with the *Renegade* staff's unanimous opinion: "Nothing, we feel, can justify the burning of books, even if they're controversial"—and an invitation for opposing views.

By the time classes started, there were only a few *Renegade*s left, but the bin of *Telegraph*s—the *Telegraph* hadn't mentioned the burning—was almost a third full. "Newspaper war!" Terry chortled as he and Jamie walked to their first class. "I love it!"

"Neat issue," Cindy said, passing them in the hall, "if I do say so myself."

But Jamie was silent, and she remained silent until lunchtime, when she and the others got their food and settled down at their usual table. It was true that she'd seen more *Renegade*s in students' hands than *Telegraph*s, and people had come up to her in each of her classes, praising the *Renegade* and saying they agreed with the lead article. But you can look at that both ways, she thought: a lot of kids haven't said anything. She'd passed Brandon Tomkins and his friends on her way into the lunchroom; there was no laughter this time, but one of them muttered something that sounded like "Now you've really done it."

"I think," Jamie said when the others, except for Nomi, who was eating with Clark at the next table, were all there, "that we need to do an opinion survey."

Terry groaned. "That's our editor. Work, work, work! Geeze, we've just done a *Renegade* issue! 'Published occasionally,' it says. It's not a frigging daily!"

"I don't mean for the *Renegade*," Jamie said quickly, watching Nomi, who was obviously listening. "I mean for the *Telegraph*, to find out what kids really think about the book burning."

"That's a great idea," said Cindy. "I'll help interview."

"We'll need photos . . ." But then Tessa's eagerness faded. "Hinchley will never approve."

"We could do it first and ask for approval afterward," Jack suggested. "That seems to be our usual M.O. anyway. We don't usually ask for approval *before* we do a story."

Nomi leaned toward them. "Yes, we do. We always planned issues in advance with Matt."

"In a general way, though," Jamie said. "We've also done a couple of stories without discussing them first, when things have come up." She pushed her chair back. "I'm going to see if I can make an announcement. We've got about half the school here right now." And before she could acknowledge her own nervousness, she walked briskly to the corner table at which the teacher-monitor sat—Jamie recognized that day's as a new student teacher—to ask permission.

"Announcement about what?" he asked, but when Jamie told him it was for the paper, he said, "Sure," and went back to correcting a pile of what looked like freshman math tests.

More aware of her nervousness now, she returned to the newspaper table and shouted, "Hey, everyone! Announcement. Can you listen for a second? Won't take long."

The racket in the room subsided, and Jamie spoke over the remaining muted voices and clatter. "You all know what happened Halloween night." There was an interested murmur. "And you all know what we've said about it in the *Renegade Telegraph*, those of you who've read it, anyway. But we still have our regular school paper, which I think should also cover the story. We'd like to try to do a sort of student-in-the-halls survey and see if we can get approval to run it in the regular *Telegraph*. If we can't, we'll run it in the *Renegade*. The basic question is 'What do you think about the book burning?' Please give your answer to Terry or Tessa or Cindy or Jack or me."

"Or me," Nomi said quietly, moving to the newspaper table and sitting down after a quick glance at Clark. "I'm still part of the *Telegraph*. And some kids might feel more comfortable talking to me. Besides, I'd still like to make up for that op-ed I didn't do. I'm not an ogre, Jamie."

"No, you're not," Jamie said quickly. "Or Nomi," she announced loudly. "You can give your answer to Nomi, too. We'd like to get some photos also, so if you don't mind having your picture taken, go to Tessa."

"Are you going to ask teachers, too?" someone asked.

Jamie looked toward the others, who nodded. "Sure. Why not? Maybe some parents and other people as well."

Karen Hodges, who Jamie now saw was sitting in the back near Sam and Brandon, jumped to her feet. "How come you're so worked up about this whole thing?" she asked. "I mean, it's just books, and they owned the ones they burned. Or is it . . ." She paused and took a step forward. "Or is it the subject matter you're upset about? Your *newspaper*"—she said the word sarcastically—"said most of the books were about homosexuality. Who cares, then, except maybe homosexuals?"

Jamie heard Nomi draw her breath in sharply, and there was some boisterous laughter from the group at Karen's table. The teacher-monitor looked up from his papers, but then looked down again. Ernie, Jamie noticed, was sitting very still two tables away with Vicky, looking as if he was barely breathing.

"Burning books is an act of censorship," Jamie called out evenly, trying to ignore the now-familiar chill that crept over her. She tried to ignore Terry, too, who'd gotten up and was standing beside her, and Nomi, who looked embarrassed, horrified, and frightened, all at the same time. Cindy and Jack looked both embarrassed and surprised. "At least *I* think it is. It's against the First Amendment. That's freedom of speech and of the press. It's against democracy. It doesn't matter what the subject matter is."

"Oh, yeah?" Brandon shouted over the heads of the students between Karen and Jamie. "If they'd burned books that were *against* homosexuality, would you have felt the same way?"

"Yes. I'd feel that way about burning any book. But what we want to find out is how all of you feel."

"You know how I feel," said Karen. "And lots of other kids feel the same way."

"Homosexuality is wrong," Al Checkers shouted. "You know that, Jamie. It's even in the Bible . . ."

The teacher-monitor looked up again, then got uncertainly to his feet.

"I agree with Al." Karen Hodges moved toward Jamie, shouting. "I don't have to wait for any survey to say it. My opinion is that it's a good thing they burned those books. I don't think we should have filth in our library, like Mrs. Buel says." She reached Jamie and, glancing at the teacher-monitor, lowered her voice. "And I don't think we should have filthy people in our school."

"Who . . ." Jamie began angrily.

Almost simultaneously, the teacher-monitor called out, "Cool it, kids. Let's not get carried away. Period's almost over anyway. Time to pack up." He waved his hand ineffectually in their direction and gathered his papers. The buzz of general lunchroom conversation resumed as students began leaving, but Karen was still facing Jamie, hands defiantly on hips, at the newspaper table.

"A lot of help he is," Terry said in a low voice, glancing after the teacher-monitor as he left. "Let it go, Jamie. Let it go."

Jamie closed her eyes for a second, trying to regain control of herself. "Can we print what you just said, Karen?" she asked when she trusted her voice.

Karen shrugged. "Like I told you, I don't have to wait for

your survey to say what I feel. But sure, if you want. Go ahead. But I bet you won't."

"Of course we will," Jamie answered, "if you repeat it to one of us later so we can write it down accurately. Remember," she said, raising her voice above the noise of departing students, "we're not sure if we can run this in the *Telegraph*. We'll try. But if we can't, we will run it in the *Renegade*, so watch for the next issue. Anyway, thanks for listening, everyone. And please give us your opinions."

Karen walked back to her table, and quickly, before anyone else could speak, Jamie sat down.

Tessa's dark skin looked ashen. "That bitch! What do you mean we'll print what she said? Where I come from," she added, her voice shaking with barely controlled fury, "we call that hate speech."

"I guess that's what we're going to have to call it here, too," said Jamie. She felt so drained that the fact that Tessa—Tessa, who was straight—was angry barely registered. "But we're also going to have to print it. If we do an opinion survey, we've got to cover all opinion, especially in the *Telegraph*."

"She's right, Tessa," Jack said calmly. "Even though what Karen said sucks. I don't care if anyone's gay or straight," he said, crumpling his sandwich wrapper and looking everywhere but at Jamie, "just so they're a good person."

"Yeah." Cindy put her hand over Jack's for a moment. "Neither do I."

"But stuff like what Karen said is harmful, for God's sake!" Tessa shouted angrily. "Like that old thing about free speech not letting people yell 'fire' in a crowded theater. Free speech doesn't let you do that. And free speech shouldn't include printing stuff that'll hurt people."

"Free speech," Jamie said, seeing Nomi watching her intently, "means everyone's allowed to voice their opinion. I can say what I want in an editorial, and other people can refute it in an op-ed or a letter. But if we do an opinion survey, it's going to cover *all* opinion, hateful or not."

"Yeah?" Tessa said acidly. "Well, then you can count me out of it, Madame Editor. I don't work for dictators, and I don't believe in giving people like Karen Hodges a public forum." Angrily, she got up from the table and stalked out of the cafeteria.

By the end of the day, Jamie had a handful of scrawled opinion statements from students, including Karen—and no word from Tessa, who had avoided her in the one class they shared after lunch. At dismissal, Terry handed her more statements, and she found an envelope on her newspaper office desk with even more. There were no notes about photos, though, and Tessa was nowhere to be found.

Miserably, Jamie walked home alone, and spent the evening sorting the statements. First Nomi, she kept thinking bitterly, now Tessa. How come Terry's the only friend I seem to be able to keep?

The next day was the same. When Jamie arrived at school that morning, she saw Tessa in the hall, but when she went up to her and said, "Hi," Tessa turned and said noncommittally, "Hey—sorry—I've got to get to class."

"Tessa . . ." Jamie began.

But she was gone.

At lunchtime Tessa wasn't in her usual place at the newspaper table.

"You're not eating," Terry chided Jamie gently after about fifteen minutes.

"No. I'm not hungry."

"She'll get over it."

"Yeah." Jamie picked up her tray. "But I won't till I find her."

"What's with our editor?" Jamie heard Cindy ask as she tossed her uneaten lunch in the trash, but she didn't wait for Terry's reply. Instead, she scoured the school, and finally found Tessa out behind the parking lot, sitting under a tree next to her backpack, smoking a cigarette.

"You don't smoke," Jamie said, standing awkwardly in front of her.

"No." Tessa stubbed the cigarette out. "You're right, Jamie, I . . ."

"Tessa," said Jamie quickly, "I *am* a dictator sometimes, you're right. I pretty much railroaded everyone into doing that survey, but I really do believe we have to publish everyone's opinions, at least about the act of burning books. We can limit it to that; that's all we asked about. But maybe even the other stuff people said wouldn't be hate speech if it was published as part of a survey, or . . ."

Tessa made a rueful sound halfway between a laugh and a sigh. "I've really been trying to understand your point, Jamie. And I guess I finally do. But still, if I say all blacks have tiny brains, or all Hispanics are crooks, or all gays molest children, that's a bunch of lies, and it's hate speech, no matter where it appears."

Jamie closed her eyes for a moment. "Okay, maybe you're right about that. It's hate*ful* speech, anyway. But I still think that if we're doing an opinion survey, we have to publish all opinions, much as I'm against hate speech and lies and bigotry and anything like them. Maybe hate speech itself is a matter of degree, sort of, and circumstance. Maybe. Maybe it's hate speech only when it causes violence—I don't know. But I do know we have to keep our personal feelings out of this. I— look." Jamie felt her mouth go suddenly dry. "What Karen said hurt me, hurt me personally, I mean, more than I can say, and . . ." She stopped, cutting herself off.

"I know, Jamie." Tessa put her hand on Jamie's arm, then almost as quickly removed it and took a few steps back. "It hurt me personally, too," she said quietly. "For you. For Terry. And I'm sorry I walked away. Look, I don't know how to say this, but Cindy told me what she and Jack think, and I think they're right. I've thought it for quite a while, but you didn't seem to want me to know, so I . . ." She paused for a moment. "You're gay, too, aren't you? Like—like Terry."

Speechless, scared, as still as if the world had iced over or as if she'd been frozen within it, Jamie nodded.

"I'm not gay," Tessa said gently. "But I—I love you, Jamie. You're one of the finest people I've ever met, maybe even the finest. And I've seen how you look when Brandon makes his cracks, and I was pretty sure what Karen was thinking that day in the john. I hate it when people are cruel, and that's what hate speech is, and that's why I was so mad."

Jamie nodded; she still couldn't speak, and she needed all her energy to keep breathing and to keep back the tears she felt welling up in her eyes. She knew she'd be touched later by what Tessa had said about loving her, but even so, the words *"I'm not gay"* sounded so final they pounded over and over in her mind, pushing away the tiny spark of hope she hadn't dared acknowledge she'd been fostering.

175

But Tessa was coming toward her now, holding out her hands, taking Jamie's, squeezing them. "I want to be your friend, Jamie. I want to go on being your friend, always, no matter what. And I'm sorry I got so mad."

Jamie squeezed Tessa's hands back and tried very hard to smile.

SEVENTEEN

"No," said Ms. Hinchley Wednesday afternoon in the newspaper office. "Absolutely not. We are not going to do anything on the book-burning story. By the time the next issue comes out, it'll be old news."

"Just look at what we've got, Ms. Hinchley," Jamie said, trying to speak calmly. She'd been up most of the night working on the survey and then writing her next *Telegraph* editorial—thankful, really, that she had those tasks to do. "We're not covering it as news; I know it'll be old by the next issue. We're covering it as reaction."

Ms. Hinchley sighed, and with a great show of reluctance took the sheets Jamie handed her while Tessa, Terry, Jack, and Cindy watched.

STUDENTS (AND OTHERS) IN THE HALLS
A Survey in Reaction to the Halloween Book Burning

After a brief introduction reiterating the facts, the survey went on to say:

We interviewed a hundred people, both at school and around town, to try to put together a representative range of opinion. Forty-eight were against the book burning, thirty-seven were for it, and fifteen weren't sure where they stood or had no opinion. A lot of people didn't want to give their names, and lack of space prevents us from printing anywhere near all the replies, so we've decided to print excerpts instead, anonymously. If anyone feels slighted and/or would like to be identified, please send us a letter about that and we'll do our best to include it in the next issue.

—Jamie Crawford, Editor in Chief

PRO

Families for Traditional Values burned their own property and they had a right to do that . . . It's a good thing they burned those books. We shouldn't have filthy books in our libraries . . . FTV had a permit for a beach bonfire, so what they did was legal . . . If it takes a bonfire to wake people up to the dangerous goings-on in our schools, well, then maybe that's what it takes . . . I'm proud of FTV. It's about time someone took a stand about obscenity and wrongheadedness in Wilson's libraries . . . If adults want to read the trash that's in the library promoting homosexuality, okay, but keep those books out of the schools and out of kids' hands. I'm grateful to Lisa Buel.

CON

Nazis burned books in World War II to suppress ideas they didn't agree with. The First Amendment says we have free speech and freedom of the press. Burning books doesn't go along with that . . . Books are ideas. If you burn a book, you burn an idea, and we need all the ideas we can get . . . Libraries have procedures for requesting removal of books. FTV should have followed them . . . I don't think communication in Wilson has failed enough to warrant an extreme measure like the one FTV took on Halloween night . . . What right does FTV have to tell me what I'm allowed to read? Only my parents have that right, and they say I'm old enough to decide for myself.

Ms. Hinchley sighed when she'd finished reading. "I have to admit you kids did a good job with this," she said, with obvious reluctance. "Very professional . . ."

"But?" said Cindy.

"But you have to remember this is a school paper, not a big-city daily or even a small-town weekly."

"Mr. Bartholomew seems to think it's okay," Jamie said quietly. "When I asked him for a quote, I told him we were planning to run a representative sample of school and town opinion in the paper. He didn't say we couldn't."

"No." Ms. Hinchley reached for the phone. "But did he know exactly what you were planning to do? Did he see the quotes?"

"No," Jack said. "But . . ."

"Mr. Bartholomew?" Ms. Hinchley said into the receiver, holding up her hand for silence. "This is Ms. Hinchley. I'm calling you from the newspaper office. Jamie has just shown me the piece she and the other editors want to run in reaction to FTV's book burning, and . . . I see . . . Well, my fear is that what they've actually gathered will further polarize an already polarized school community, and . . . I see. Yes, I will . . . All right . . . Yes, right away. Thank you. Goodbye."

Ms. Hinchley turned to face them. "Mr. Bartholomew would like to see the whole survey."

"I'll take it," Jamie offered.

Terry held out his hand. "No, I'll take it, Jamie. You've still got to show her the editorial."

"Editorial?" Ms. Hinchley raised her eyebrows as Terry left, followed by Jack and Cindy. Cindy whispered "Good luck" to Jamie as she passed her.

"Right. Editorial," Jamie said, nodding her thanks to the others. "Look, this is the hottest thing going, in town as well as in school. We can't just ignore it or pretend it didn't happen. And if we're any kind of newspaper at all, we have to run an editorial on it. People expect that!"

Ms. Hinchley sighed again. "I really think this is a grave mistake. Let's see it, Jamie."

Tessa got up and stood behind Jamie's chair as Jamie handed the editorial to Ms. Hinchley.

Editorial
HALLOWEEN BOOK BURNING

The Halloween book burning brings home how very fragile our democracy may be—and also how very strong. On the one hand, burning books seems a blatant violation of free speech and of the right to publish and distribute the written word—freedom of the press.

On the other hand, burning books seems to be a form of free speech in itself, if one takes it as symbolic speech.

The Supreme Court ruled some years ago that burning the American flag is a constitutionally protected act of political speech. Isn't book burning the same thing?

I can see both arguments pretty clearly, I think—and yet I have to come down on the side that says burning books is wrong. Maybe it can be considered constitutionally protected speech, and as such, I should, if not applaud it, at least refrain from saying it should be outlawed. So I'll say that: it shouldn't be outlawed.

But that doesn't mean I have to like it.

Let's face it, FTV doesn't approve of AIDS education, factual information about homosexuality, and making condoms available in the nurse's office; that's why they burned those books. If parents don't want their kids to learn something or to read something, then those parents should do what they can to ensure that their kids don't. But it isn't right for those parents to deprive other people's kids of that information. If we had only one set of ideas in this country, we'd be a nation of sheep, not people, and that can lead to the kind of thing that happened in Nazi Germany. They burned books there, too.

Is it right to hide information from Wilson's kids just because FTV doesn't approve of it?

I don't think so—and I think that's what this argument is all about.

"No, Jamie," said Ms. Hinchley. "I admit that it's well written and well thought out, but it's also inflammatory. And there's no place for that in a school paper."

Jamie's hands balled up into fists. "Why not?" she asked, fighting to keep her temper.

"Because a school paper's main job, as I've said a hundred times before, is to bring a school together, not drive it apart."

"But it's already apart! The damage has been done. You're asking me to sweep it under the rug and pretend it never happened. What do you want me to write? An editorial about needing more tampons in the girls' bathroom? No, sorry. That would be too sexy. A bland one about—about a shortage of straws in the lunchroom, maybe, or—or what to wear to a football game? That's not the kind of writer I am, and it's not the kind of paper Matt Caggin wants the *Telegraph* to be, either!"

Furious, Jamie snatched her editorial off Ms. Hinchley's desk, brushed past Tessa, and stormed out of the office, where she stopped, angry tears flooding her eyes, and leaned against the wall. "Damn her," she muttered under her breath. "Damn her, damn her, damn her!"

In a moment, Tessa was beside her. "You're going to get yourself suspended. Hinchley turned a lot whiter than she already is, and when she picked up the phone again, her hand was shaking."

"I don't care if I get expelled!" Jamie shouted. "Hinchley's a stupid, timid excuse for a human being. I bet her entire house is pink . . ."

"Pale pink," said Tessa, "with ruffles around the shutters . . ."

"Snow-white ruffles . . ."

"White lilies outside on the lawn, with tiny little deer lawn ornaments, and . . ."

"And elves. Lots of elves. Smiling. When it rains, they smile. When it snows, they smile. When there's a hurricane, they smile . . . Tess." Jamie almost took her hand, then thought better of it. "Thank you."

"You're welcome. What are you going to do now?"

"I don't know."

"You're not going to give up, are you?"

"I don't know."

"Jamie Crawford, you are not going to give up!"

"No," Jamie said tiredly, "no, I guess I'm not. The survey really does belong in the *Telegraph*. But what am I going to do?"

"Bargain."

"Bargain?"

"Bargain."

"Yeah," Jamie said. "Yeah. Maybe if I could get an op-ed . . ."

"Nomi."

"Oh, right," Jamie said sarcastically. "Perfect."

"No, really. It's worth a try. She said she wanted to make up for not doing one before. Or maybe you could ask Clark."

Jamie considered it briefly. "Yeah, maybe Clark. I don't want to push Nomi too hard." She thought a minute longer, then waved the editorial, which was still crumpled in her hand. "Bartholomew. I'll show him the editorial. If he over-rules Hinchley, we're in." She turned and began striding down the hall.

Tessa ran after her, matching her steps to Jamie's. "*If*," she said. "Maybe," she added when they were outside Mr. Bartholomew's office, "see what he says about the survey piece first . . ."

Terry was just coming out. "It's okay!" he shouted jubi-lantly, his eyes shining for the first time since Ernie's decision about Vicky. "He says it's a great piece and he wishes the school had a Pulitzer, because we'd get it."

"All right!" exclaimed Tessa.

"He may withdraw that," Jamie said, knocking, "when he sees what I'm going to ask him next."

EIGHTEEN

Mr. Bartholomew's face was impassive while he read Jamie's editorial. When he'd finished, he gazed out his window for so long that Jamie thought she'd scream. But when he finally turned to her, he was smiling—a bit wanly, but smiling.

"Jamie Crawford," he said, "I'm glad you're a senior, because pretty soon there's going to be no stopping you. As I said to Terry, I wish we had a Pulitzer to give. This"—he picked up the editorial—"is fine work, mature, well expressed, dramatic, persuasive."

"Can we run it?"

Mr. Bartholomew looked startled. "Say again?"

"Can we run it? Ms. Hinchley says we can't. But if we got an op-ed—I mean, I can see that; this is pretty biased, and it's a controversial issue, and . . ."

"Do you think you can get an op-ed? Remember what happened with the condom editorial."

"I know, but—yeah. I think I can get one this time." Jamie hesitated. "Especially if you'll let us run this if we can get one."

"Yes, I will. I suspect the school committee will object—it does go against their edict about editorials. But this is a vital issue, and it's always been my feeling that, barring obscenity and libel, freedom of the press applies to school papers, too. I warn you, though, there's a famous court case that doesn't entirely support that, and a good many people, including, it seems, the members of FTV, don't either. I'll argue against anyone who tries to curb the *Telegraph* more than I think is reasonable, Jamie, but there's no guarantee I'll prevail." He handed the editorial back to her.

"Thank you," Jamie said humbly. She wondered if the school committee would be able to fire him if they got upset with the editorial and the survey. Maybe, she thought, we shouldn't do it after all. Maybe it's too risky to too many people . . .

But before she could say anything, Mr. Bartholomew started punching buttons on his phone. "I'll take care of Ms. Hinchley." He gestured to the door, obviously asking Jamie to leave.

The next day, Mr. Bartholomew called the newspaper editors, plus Jack and Cindy, into his office and announced that Ms. Hinchley had "graciously agreed" to advise the freshman literary magazine and so wouldn't be able to continue on the paper. He was looking for another adviser, he said, but in the meantime, the paper's editors should report to him. "I don't have time to hang around your office," he told them, "and I think you've proved you're capable of running the paper yourselves. Just bring me all copy before it's final."

"That is one brave man," Jamie said as they left his office, and at the same time Terry stabbed his fist into the air, shouting "YES!" Then he threw his arms around Jamie, Tessa, Jack, Cindy, and Nomi, and they shared an awkward six-way hug.

On Monday, both the survey and Jamie's editorial ran, along with an op-ed piece written by Clark:

Op-Ed
MORE THOUGHTS ON THE BOOK BURNING

There's no question but what FTV's dramatic book burning on Halloween night has polarized this school and this town. And because of that, I can understand why some people condemn it. I agree with FTV's stand on condom distribution and sex education. And I think FTV is right that the books they burned shouldn't be available to kids. Okay, maybe they're selling us high school kids short. We're not children anymore, and we're not dumb. We're not going to be hurt by having access to other ideas, even ideas that are abhorrent to us, as the ideas in those books are. But it's not going to hurt us to have those books in a locked case either, and that will protect impressionable children, who really have no business seeing them.

The book burning was a symbol, a very dramatic one, sure, but sometimes it takes a dramatic symbol or act to bring people to their senses. The fact remains that people all over the world are dying of AIDS in great numbers, and the fact remains that teaching that homosexuality is okay is immoral, and teaching that relying on condoms will prevent AIDS is dangerous. Worse than that, using condoms to give oneself permission to have premarital sex, or to have homosexual sex, is also immoral, not to mention selfish and dangerous. Kids need to be taught to respect their bodies, to regard their bodies as temples, as the Bible says, and to cherish them enough not to abuse them. Sex is for married love between men and women and for procreation within marriage, not for sensual indulgence. We need books that teach that, and classes that teach that. If the Halloween book burning has reminded people of it—and I think it has—then it was a good thing.

"Opinion," Terry said, slipping into his place at the newspaper lunch table on Monday when the paper came out, "I'd say is running about sixty–forty now. Sixty for our side, forty for FTV's." He glanced across the room to where Ernie was sitting alone under a window, not far from where Vicky and Brandon seemed to be having an animated conversation opposite the teacher-monitor's table. Then he picked up his hamburger and took a large bite.

"That's not bad." Tessa made room for Nomi, who'd just arrived with her lunch tray.

"Good op-ed," Jamie said to Nomi.

"I thought so, too," Nomi replied. "I'm proud of Clark." She opened a can of soda. "But could we talk about something else?"

"Sure," said Jack. "Let's see . . ."

"The weather," Tessa suggested.

"Football," said Terry.

Jamie grimaced. "Math?"

"Mr. Bartholomew's new tie." Cindy put down her sandwich. "Have you noticed?"

"No." Tessa leaned forward with mock enthusiasm. "Do tell."

Terry rolled his eyes and clapped his hand to his forehead. "Not," he said dramatically, "the one with the naked woman on it!"

"No, no," said Cindy. "The one with the eensy-weensy cute bunnies on it."

"And the socks." Tessa winked at Jamie. "The matching socks."

Terry picked up his lunch tray. "Excuse me. I've got to go barf."

Instead, though, he headed toward Ernie.

All afternoon Jamie kept sneaking glances at people in the halls and in her classes to see if they were reading the paper and, if so, what they were reading. "Your eyes are positively on stalks," Tessa whispered as they walked to social studies. "It's like you're staring at everyone, everyone's papers, anyway."

"Look. There's another *Telegraph*, open once again, ladies and gents, to the editorial page."

"Yeah," said Tessa, "and the hands that are holding it, if you'll swing your eyes upward, oh, editor, belong to Karen Hodges, our favorite sophomore. Hi, Karen," she said cheerfully when Karen turned and looked at them.

"Oh. Hi."

"What do you think?" Jamie asked her.

Karen briefly looked more startled than hostile. "Think? About what?"

"Of what you're reading, bonehead," Tessa answered. "Of the editorials."

"One sucks and the other's okay. And if you want to know which is which," Karen added, sashaying down the hall as the bell rang, "yours is the one that sucks, Jamie Crawford."

"Predictable," said Jamie, trying not to mind.

"Well," Tessa said, "at least she's honest. Come on. We're going to be late."

Social studies was uneventful, mostly, except Terry handed Jamie a note saying, "Meet me and Ernie—YES, ERNIE!—at Sloan's Beach after school?" Jamie gave him a thumbs-up sign across the room, but when the bell rang she was delayed by a girl who came up to her saying, "Hey, Jamie, good editorial this week," and a boy with her who added, "It's good you, like, had two, one pro and one con. That was cool. You should do that more, you know? I've been thinking of writing for the paper myself, maybe."

By the time Jamie had taken down his name and found out that what he really wanted to do was publish what he called "satiric political poetry" in the paper, Terry had left.

Tiredness washed over her as she hurried down to the seniors' lockers in the basement. Maybe, she thought, I can ask Terry if I can meet them some other time.

But when she got to the basement she saw that Terry was standing near her locker with Ernie, and it was very obvious something was wrong. Terry looked furious, and Ernie looked stunned, defeated.

"What's up?" Jamie reached nervously for her combination lock.

"Um, Jamie, you sure you want to do that?" Terry said. "You sure you've got anything in there that you really need tonight?"

"Yes, I'm sure." Jamie looked from one to the other of them, puzzled. "Books, my jacket—what's with you guys, anyway?" She twirled her lock and pulled open the door.

The words hit her full in the face when she picked up the thin sheet of cardboard that fluttered down. They were spelled out in big black capital letters, spray-painted on both sides of the cardboard:

FUCKING DYKE SLUT LOVER

"Oh, Lord," Jamie said. "Oh, no."

"We got love notes, too," Terry told her. "Ernie and I also got little presents, taped to the outside of our lockers." He displayed a package of condoms, crumpled pink wrapping paper, and a gift tag: *For Wilson High's Number One Fag*.

"I'm Number Two Fag," Ernie said with a thin smile, his voice shaking.

NINETEEN

They all got into Terry's car, squeezing into the front seat.

"Brandon Tomkins." Terry turned the key in the ignition. "I bet. Brandon and his buddies, Al and Sam . . ."

"Sam's only a sophomore," said Jamie.

"Yeah." Terry gunned the car angrily as he backed it up. "But he's Brandon's cousin or something. He acts like he is, anyway. Maybe he's got a crush on him. Maybe we should send *him* a note."

"What are we going to do?" Jamie asked.

"Maybe nothing," Terry said. "Don't give them the satisfaction."

"We could report them," Ernie suggested. "I'm sure it was Brandon." His voice was calm now, but very quiet. "And probably Al and Sam. And Karen. I guess word got around—I broke up with Vicky," he added, turning to Jamie.

Jamie, surprised, glanced over at Terry, who nodded, grinning. "So that's why . . ."

"That's why we asked you to meet us," Terry said. "So we could tell you." He looked happier than Jamie had ever seen him, despite the notes in their lockers.

"I had to do it," Ernie explained. "It—it was crazy for me to go out with her. Crazy. I tried to like, you know, touching her, but . . . It was no good. She's really nice, but I kept thinking of how much I really wanted to be with Terry. Who I want to love," he added carefully. "Who I do love." He put his hand on the back of Terry's neck; Jamie saw Terry reach up and squeeze it.

She turned away, looking out the window.

"We can't let it get to us." Terry pulled the car into the parking lot at Sloan's Beach. "Those signs and stuff. If we do, it'll get worse."

"Ms. Hinchley would approve of not reacting," Jamie said wryly.

Ernie went silently to the edge of the lot, where he stood staring out over the water. Low, easy swells rolled toward shore, breaking gently on the rocks; a few herring gulls called raucously to each other in the chill November air.

"He hasn't told me anything about him and Vicky except what he just said in the car," Terry said in an undertone to Jamie. Then he went to Ernie, put his arm around him, and for a moment they talked quietly.

Jamie watched them both as they walked back. "It's hard doing nothing," she said carefully, not wanting to intrude on their privacy by asking more about Vicky. "It's our move," she went on. "They must be waiting to see what we'll do. If we refuse to play, it won't be fun for them anymore. Maybe they'll just drop it."

"Maybe," Ernie said, his eyes still on Terry. "But what if they don't?"

Terry thrust his hands into his jacket pockets. "If they don't, then we should do something more active," he said. "You know, fight back. As soon as they do something else."

They didn't have long to wait. The next morning was quiet, except for curious glances and a few snickers, which Jamie tried her best to ignore. Ernie looked dazed as he moved through the halls, and Terry's face was set and grim. Jamie considered telling Tessa, but decided against it; it didn't seem fair to involve her or any of the others.

But at lunch, when Brandon shot them a couple of loud fag jokes as he passed the newspaper table, Cindy said, "Wow, Brandon's in fine form today. What's going on?" and Tessa, eyebrows raised, turned to Jamie. "Anything happening that the rest of us should know about?" she asked—and Terry explained.

"Shut up, Brandon," Cindy called as Brandon passed again, firing another salvo, and Brandon called back, "Watch out who you associate with, babe. They say people are known by the company they keep."

Jack made a face. "Yeah, that's right, Brandon. Look at the lowlife you've got around you. Phew!"

"Easy," Terry told them. "Let it go."

Nomi, Jamie noticed, had sat rigidly in her chair during the whole exchange; she and Clark were having lunch together, as they'd often done recently, but today they were several tables away.

The taunts continued all week, and on Thursday morning, there were lavender bows on their lockers—Jamie's, Terry's, Ernie's, and, this time, also Tessa's. "Kind of pretty," Terry remarked, removing his. "I'd almost like to keep it."

"Why not?" Jamie said, but she ripped Tessa's off angrily, glad she wasn't there to see it. Terry put his back.

Ernie walked away.

Terry thrust two sheets of copy paper into Jamie's hand. "Sports feature," he said, and went after Ernie. Jamie nodded, and decided she had just enough time to drop the feature off before classes started, so she went to the newspaper office and unlocked the door, then stooped to pick up an envelope that lay on the floor, as if someone had slid it underneath. On it was written:

TO THE DYKE EDITOR OF THE SCHOOL FAG RAG

Her hands shaking, she put Terry's feature on her desk and ripped open the envelope:

TO THE DYKE EDITOR OF THE SCHOOL FAG RAG:
WARNING!
This school doesn't like what you're doing. You are IN DANGER. You had better stop publishing so much filthy pro-homosexual sicko queer stuff in your paper. We DON'T LIKE IT!
If you and your queer staff don't watch out, you will be in BIG TROUBLE!
THIS IS NOT A JOKE!

The Straight Majority

It was all Jamie could do to sit through her first class, and she spent the whole period alternating between rage and fear. But by the time the period ended, she'd made up her mind what she wanted to do, and she hurried down the hall to the principal's office, where she plunked the letter down on Mr. Bartholomew's desk. "I'd like to print it," she said, "because I'd like people to see how sick some kids are. If we don't print it, whoever wrote it will go around saying we're cowards or something."

Mr. Bartholomew shook his head. "I don't think it's a good idea to print it, Jamie."

"I was afraid you might say that. But . . ."

"Then I don't need to explain."

"Well, yeah, maybe you do." She sat down.

"It's my old argument about the school's being polarized. I don't want to risk making that worse. Let me handle this, okay? It's pretty obvious what the source of it is. And I think we can make sure those threats aren't carried out. Let me keep the letter." He paused. "Jamie? Okay?"

Jamie hesitated. But she realized there really wasn't anything more she could do. "Okay," she said reluctantly.

Mr. Bartholomew smiled. "Good. As a matter of fact, there's already something that I think may help. I've just arranged for a special speaker to come the week before Thanksgiving to try to calm things down, or at least make people think twice before they hit out at other people. He does workshops about prejudice. In fact"—Mr. Bartholomew gestured toward a table under his window, on which lay a pile of white cardboard oblongs covered with blue lettering—"I'm about to ask for volunteers to put up some posters. Do you think you and your friends might . . ."

"Okay." Jamie took the posters, and tried to hide the fact that she was still boiling mad.

And underneath that, scared.

Early Friday morning, Jamie met Terry outside school, and by the time the first bell rang, the whole school was papered with posters:

PEACE TO ALL

The Pre-Thanksgiving Assembly Will Be Devoted to
Bringing Wilson High's Diverse Communities Together:
Male, Female, Black, White, Gay, Straight
All Religions, All Nationalities
Let Us Bury Hate and Become a Whole School Again
Safe for All
Friendly to All
SPEAKER: HOWARD ARNOLD
COME ONE, COME ALL!

By lunchtime, all the posters had been torn down.

"We'll make more," Jamie said grimly. "And we'll keep making them and putting them up for as long as we have to."

But next time, the assembly posters were replaced by huge ones with stark black letters on red oaktag:

THE EVIL IN WILSON
A FORUM

TIME: WEDNESDAY, NOVEMBER 16
7:00 P.M.
PLACE: MEETING ROOM
LORD'S ASSEMBLY CHURCH

EVERYONE WELCOME!
WE MUST DEVELOP STRATEGIES FOR FIGHTING THE
EVIL
THAT HAS COME TO OUR COMMUNITY
IN THE FORM OF OBSCENE BOOKS,

"Two can play that game," Terry said angrily, reaching for a poster.

But Jamie pulled his hand back. "Forget it. I don't think Mr. Bartholomew will let these posters stay, anyway. It's not a school event."

Jamie, it turned out, was right. But the "Evil in Wilson" posters soon appeared all over town, even though they were banned from school property. The pre-Thanksgiving assembly posters were torn down once more, until Mr. Bartholomew called Brandon, Al, and Sam into his office and threatened to suspend them—and finally, on November 16, Wilson's students crowded into the auditorium and heard the speaker talk about prejudice and cruelty, diversity and love. Matt Caggin was there, sitting with Mr. Bartholomew; and Cindy and Jack, in the front row, applauded especially loudly at every possible opportunity—almost, Jamie thought, as if they were trying to lead the others in the audience.

But after the meeting, when she and Terry and Ernie went to Terry's car, there was a piece of paper folded under the driver's side windshield wiper. FAG SINNERS REPENT! it said. REPENT OR MEET YOUR DOOM!

TWENTY

At lunch Monday, Brandon, Al, and Sam whistled as Terry and Ernie walked into the cafeteria; Tessa, Jamie, and the others were already at their table. "Ooooh," Brandon called in falsetto, "aren't they sweet?"

"The lovebirds," Al called. Sam cooed, and several people laughed loudly and whistled.

Suddenly Tessa shoved her chair back and leaped to her feet. "Some people," she shouted, "are so dumb they have no idea what's funny and what isn't. I didn't know we had so many Neanderthals in this school."

"Hey, Jamie," Brandon called, "can't you control your girl-friend?"

Tessa pushed her chair into the table so hard she toppled it.

Jamie put her hand on Tessa's arm. "Tess, leave it," she said, glancing toward the teacher-monitor's table; it was empty, and she remembered seeing one of the secretaries beckoning the teacher-monitor out a few minutes earlier. "It's better to ignore them. Except," she added, "we'd better get one thing cleared up. Sorry to disappoint you, Brandon," she called, "but I don't have a girlfriend."

"Can't even make it as a dyke, huh, butch?" Brandon called back. "Maybe you need lessons from a real man."

"That sure wouldn't be you, Brandon!" Tessa shouted.

"Enough," Jack said quietly. "You'd better let it go. Don't get him any madder. Truce, man," he called to Brandon. "Why waste everyone's time? Who cares, you know?"

But Brandon pushed his chair back and sauntered toward them, toward Jamie, right up to her, put his hand out, open, ran it over her cheek . . .

Jack stood up, but it was Terry who grabbed Brandon's shoulder. "That's enough, Brandon." Terry stepped between him and Jamie. "That's enough."

Brandon whirled, his fists clenched. "I love it! I really love it. The fag comes to help the dyke. Geeze, Gage, I don't think I better hit you. I mean, that'd be like hitting a girl, and . . ."

Terry's fist shot out and caught Brandon on the chin, sending him to the floor.

Instantly the other boys at Brandon's table rushed in, grabbing Terry and bending him facedown over the back of a chair.

"Let him go!" Ernie shouted, running toward Brandon. But Sam Mills pushed Ernie into a chair and held him there.

Tessa stepped quickly between Jamie and the boys. "Get out of here," she said to Jamie, her voice low and urgent. "Get out of here and find a teacher, any teacher. This is going to turn really nasty."

But Jamie couldn't move.

"Look at that pretty fag butt!" One of Brandon's friends pointed to Terry's rear end as Brandon slowly got up from the floor. "Isn't that cute?"

"Cute as heck," said another boy. "I think we need to fix it up some, though, don't you?"

Out of the corner of her eye Jamie saw everyone in the cafeteria watching, saw someone from the kitchen staff emerge, saw Tessa run out of the room—as Brandon, rubbing his chin, said, "Yeah. We need to fix both fag butts." He grabbed Terry under one arm; Al Checkers grabbed him under the other. Sam and another boy yanked Ernie to his feet.

"Brandon, no!" Vicky shouted—but Jamie's voice was louder. "Let them go!" she yelled, elbowing her way past Jack and Clark, who were heading toward the boys. "Let them go!" She saw as she moved that Nomi and Cindy were motionless, their faces frozen in horror.

"Oh, mercy," said Brandon in a squeaky-high voice. "It's the dyke editor." He dropped his voice. "You might as well come along, too. See what real men can do." With his free hand, he grabbed Jamie's arm, wrenching it painfully behind her back, and pictures of the wrestling matches he'd won for Wilson High flashed into her mind as she heard herself cry out in pain . . .

"Hang on there, Tomkins!"

The door to the hall burst open, and two teachers, followed by Mr. Bartholomew, ran in.

"What do you think you're doing, Tomkins, Mills, Checkers, the rest of you?" Mr. Bartholomew boomed at the boys. "Let go of those three instantly!"

"We were just kidding." Brandon pushed Jamie roughly away.

"Some joke." Terry, released, rubbed his shoulder and looked anxiously toward Ernie, as he, too, was let go.

"There's no way they were kidding, Mr. Bartholomew,"

Jamie gasped. "No way." She was glad to hear an assenting murmur from most of the other students.

"In my office," Mr. Bartholomew ordered, grabbing Brandon's arm. "All of you. Now. You, too," he said to Tessa, who, Jamie now saw, was standing by the door. She must have gotten him, Jamie thought gratefully.

When they reached the office, Mr. Bartholomew pushed Brandon and his cohorts inside and barked, "Find someplace to sit. I'll deal with you in a minute." He slammed the door shut and turned to Terry, Tessa, Jamie, and Ernie. "First of all, anyone hurt?"

"A little sore," said Terry, "but no, not really."

"Jamie?"

"No, I—I'm okay."

"Ernie?"

"Me, too." Ernie's face was very white. Jamie could see that he was shaking and trying hard to control it. Then she realized she was shaking, too.

"I want you to know that I will not tolerate this kind of behavior in this school. I intend to suspend the ringleaders at least till after Thanksgiving, and I intend to notify their parents. If there's anything you want to say to them or their parents, let me know. The four of you can have the rest of the day off if you want."

"There's the paper," Jamie said, cradling her throbbing arm. "We've got to work on the next issue."

"If you wish. But you don't have to go to classes."

"Yes, we do," Tessa said with a quick glance at the others. "Excuse me, but we do. If we don't, kids'll think they got to us. And that's the last thing we need."

Mr. Bartholomew sighed. "You're probably right, Tessa. I

just want you to know," he told them, "that I think you are very, very brave. I respect all of you more than I can say. But I think you'd better be careful around here from now on."

Tessa muttered something under her breath.

"What?" asked Mr. Bartholomew.

"I said 'Silence Is Death.' I don't think we can be quiet. I *know* Jamie can't be. We can't let them win, Mr. Bartholomew."

"No," said Jamie, "we can't," and Terry nodded.

"I don't want to silence you," Mr. Bartholomew told them. "But I also don't want this school to be torn apart. If Tessa hadn't come for me, I really think there could have been a riot. Let's all think about a possible solution, okay? Meanwhile, do what you have to do."

Terry looked at his watch. "What we have to do," he said, "is go to class. We're already late."

Jack and Cindy were waiting around the corner in the hall, and they walked Jamie and Terry to math class after walking Ernie to English and Tessa to biology. The other students stared, but for the first time all week, no one said anything. Jamie's head ached and she found it hard to concentrate; her arm and shoulder ached, too, from where Brandon had twisted them. Her mind felt numb, and every once in a while tears rose in her eyes, though no conscious thought had precipitated them. After math, Nomi, still looking shaken, gave Jamie a tentative smile and whispered, "Are you okay?"

"Yes, thanks," Jamie answered stiffly, but before she could say anything else, Nomi was gone.

At the end of the day, Jamie, carrying her books and her jacket, found Terry standing outside the newspaper office.

"Jamie."

Something in his voice stopped her from fishing the office key out of her pocket.

"Have you seen Ernie?" he asked tensely. "I can't find him anywhere."

"He doesn't have swim practice?"

"He *does* have swim practice. But he didn't go. And he can't be doing laps, because the team's using the pool."

"Maybe he went home after his English class?" Jamie suggested, but Terry's face made her doubt her own words even as she tried to justify them. "I mean, I don't think I'd go to swim practice either, after today. The team's not exactly what you'd call gay friendly, right? If it wasn't for the newspaper . . . What?"

Terry was shaking his head; his voice was tight, barely under control. "He wouldn't go home. His parents are too awful. Jamie, I know this has happened before and it's been okay, but would you help me look for him? Please? I'm really, really worried . . ." Terry's voice broke.

Quickly Jamie put her hand on his shoulder. "Okay. We'll go find him." She shrugged awkwardly into her jacket. "Where do you want to look?"

"The beach, I guess. Harbor, too, maybe. And the lake. I think he'd want to be . . . You know. Near water."

"Okay." Jamie followed him to his car, trying to ignore the implications of what he'd said, trying to push away the feeling that "near" probably wasn't the word he'd really meant.

They drove in silence to Sloan's Beach. It was a gray day again, and chilly; the sky and the sea were almost the same pale whitish-blue. The tide was high, with water lapping against the shore.

And standing on a rock at the edge of the sea was a small, forlorn figure, silhouetted against the sky. Next to him was a dark object—soft, draped—some kind of garment, maybe, Jamie thought as Terry sobbed, "Oh, thank God!" and they both hurried out of the car and down onto the beach.

Ernie turned to face them when they were almost there, and Jamie saw that the dark object was really a discarded jacket and sweater. Ernie was wearing just his shirt and pants; his shoes, socks tucked inside them, were neatly beside the jacket and sweater, and the bottoms of his pants legs were wet nearly to his knees.

"It's okay," he said, smiling benignly when they stopped, unsure how to approach him, what to say. "It's okay now. I'm sorry. But . . ."

With a choking sound, Terry ran to him, threw his arms around him, held him there on the rock with the gulls wheeling around and the sharp November wind blowing cold and strong, mingling his dark hair with Ernie's—blond and black strands intertwined, Jamie thought absently, picking up the jacket and sweater, shaking them out, brushing them off.

"Here." Terry took the sweater Jamie held out to him and slipped it over Ernie's head. "You must be cold; here. Jacket, too." He helped him into it, dressing him as if he were a very little boy. "Come on, we'll turn the heater on in the car, get you home. Sit down a minute; let's get something on your feet."

Obediently, Ernie sat, and Terry rolled his socks onto his feet tenderly—long white feet, they were, Jamie saw, with slender toes, neatly trimmed nails . . .

"Your feet are so cold!" Terry chafed them before putting Ernie's shoes on.

"I couldn't do it." Ernie's voice was dreamlike, but—proud, that's it, Jamie thought; he's *proud*. "I was sure I would. It was—so awful, what happened today. So horrible." He shivered, but hardly seemed to notice. Terry helped him stand, put his arm around his waist, and led him off the rock; Jamie, her arm around him, too, walked on his other side, both of them trying to warm him as they led him back to the car.

He went on talking, words pouring out of him now. "Like I told you, I tried with Vicky, even though I really knew I loved you, Terry." He took Terry's hand; Jamie could see tears glistening on his lashes. "But after I broke up with her, I wasn't sure I was brave enough to be gay. I was afraid I wouldn't have the guts, you know, with my parents and all. It felt so good, so right, to be back with you, Terry, so good not to be lying or hiding, and good that you, Jamie, were our friend; I knew we weren't really alone and I kept telling myself, Okay, I can do it; I have to do it. Then there were the things with the lockers, and today—it wasn't just me who was the target, and I kept thinking maybe it was my fault you guys were—were targets, too. If I'd stuck it out with Vicky . . ."

"If you'd stuck it out with Vicky," Terry interrupted, "like you said, you'd have been living a lie and making us both miserable. Vicky, too, eventually. And like I know I told you, Brandon's an old enemy of Jamie's and mine."

"I wanted to come back to you a couple of weeks ago, Terry," Ernie went on. "And I know I want to—to stay with you. But after today in the lunchroom . . . I was so scared, Terry, so scared!"

"Me, too." Terry hugged him.

"So was I," Jamie said. "Terrified. We'd have been stupid

not to have been scared. I don't think that's cowardly. Just sensible."

Ernie smiled wanly and shivered again; they were nearly back at the car. "Today after they almost beat us up, I kept thinking again of what everyone's been saying, and what the Bible says and my parents, and I just didn't see that there was much future in anything. It was like I couldn't be straight or gay either, you know?"

Jamie opened the passenger door. "Let's all sit in front. Ernie, you sit between us. Here, Terry, I'll drive." She got in the driver's side and switched on the ignition and the heater. "Where to, Ernie?"

"My house," Terry said quickly. "I'll lend you some clothes. It'll be okay," he added when Ernie looked alarmed. "Mom likes you, remember? So does my dad. They were glad when I told them we were together again. I think they'll be okay even if we tell them, you know, why your clothes are wet. But we can say whatever you want to say. I don't think they'll pry." Terry took Ernie's hand. "Come on, Ernie. How about it?"

Ernie hesitated, and for a minute Jamie was afraid he was going to refuse. She was about to offer to take him to her house, at least to dry off, when Ernie finally spoke.

"Okay," he said gratefully, and Jamie, relieved, backed the car out and turned it around. "Thanks. I don't think my folks would buy any explanation I could think of."

"We'll buy it, though," said Terry. "The true one, anyway. If you want to tell us the rest of it."

As she headed out of the lot and felt the heat come up, Jamie saw Ernie grip Terry's hand harder. "I took off my jacket and sweater," Ernie said without expression. "And I took off my shoes and socks, and then I thought, no, I want to be weighed down, so I picked up some stones and put them in my pockets." He let go of Terry and dug in his pockets, laying stones on the dashboard shelf. "And then I waded into the water. I didn't even feel it was cold, or that the bottom was stony and rough. And I was—I was just walking, you know, straight out, and thinking, I'm a swimmer, I have to remember not to swim, when this seagull swooped down and grabbed a fish, and I could see the fish struggling and flapping around in the gull's claws. And then the gull dropped it, or it wrenched itself free, and it fell back into the water and swam away. It looked so joyful and so—so free. It was able to be itself again, you know? And it was free to do what it was supposed to do. I thought of the joy I've felt with you, Terry, and then I thought, okay, God made the fish and He made me, too, and maybe what people are supposed to do is find out who they really are, and maybe it isn't evil and wrong as long as no one harms anyone, and . . . Well, anyway, I turned around and went back to the rock, and I felt—wonderful. Clean. Free and stronger. Not strong, but stronger.

"I'm not as strong as you two," he said as Jamie turned onto Terry's street and pulled up outside his house. "But I'm stronger than I was. Much stronger."

TWENTY-ONE

At nearly nine o'clock that night, while Jamie was doing homework and trying to ignore the aching bruises on her arms and shoulders, her mother called up to her. "Jamie! Phone! It's Nomi."

Her heart suddenly racing, Jamie picked up the extension in the upstairs hall. "Got it!" she called to her mother, and then, into the receiver, said, "Hi, Nom', what's up?"

"Oh, Jamie," Nomi said breathlessly, "I've been thinking all day about that awful thing in the cafeteria, and Clark and I have been talking about it, and Jamie, I'm so sorry! I know it's kind of late, but—well, can I come over?"

"Um—sure," Jamie said after glancing at her watch. "I guess. Okay."

By the time Nomi arrived, Jamie had told her parents she was coming, had helped Ronnie understand a lesson in using quotation marks, and had tried unsuccessfully to finish the social studies homework.

Suddenly Nomi was there, standing hesitantly at Jamie's

door. Jamie got up, and a moment later Nomi was hugging her, as if there'd never been a quarrel between them.

"Oh, Jamie," she whispered, "I can't imagine how scared you must've been today!"

"Pretty scared," Jamie said. "But I didn't really feel it till after Mr. Bartholomew came and it was over."

"If he hadn't come . . ."

"If he hadn't come," Jamie said slowly, "or if it hadn't been at school, I think they'd have dragged us someplace and raped me and made Terry and Ernie watch. And I think they'd have raped them, too, or beaten them really badly. But the important thing is that Tessa got Mr. Bartholomew and he came, and he suspended Brandon and Al and the others. So I guess . . ." She winced inwardly, thinking of Ernie on the beach. "I guess we're safe, at least for now."

"Jamie, some things . . ." Nomi's voice was low, shaking. "I couldn't think of much else today, like I said. I—oh, Lord, I don't know." Nomi covered her face with her hands and sank down onto Jamie's bed.

Jamie sat beside her, gently rubbing her back. "What is it, Nom'? What?"

Nomi took her hands down; her eyes were brimming with tears. "I believe in my religion. I believe in God and Jesus and the Bible, and that what the Bible says is right. And, forgive me, Jamie, I believe homosexuality is wrong. But the Bible says to hate the sin and love the sinner, and I do love you, Jamie; I always have. I wish you weren't a—a . . ."

"A lesbian," Jamie said quietly, though her hands were sweating and her heart was racing again.

"A lesbian. You are, aren't you? It's true what Karen Hodges and Brandon and all of them say, isn't it?"

Slowly, Jamie nodded. "I think so, Nomi. At least I'm pretty sure. Tessa isn't, by the way. We're . . ." Jamie cleared her throat. "She knows about me, but we're—we're just friends."

Nomi closed her eyes for a moment. "I kept wishing you weren't a—you know. But I guess I've known it for a long time, sensed it, anyway, even before this year. I didn't think it was true back when we were younger, but now— Well, Clark's wondered, too; we've talked about it. And we talked about it a lot today. At first I thought it meant you'd changed, but you haven't. You're a fine, strong person, Jamie. That doesn't fit with what I've always thought about—lesbians."

"I guess lesbians are like anyone else, Nomi. Some good, some bad. Like some fat and some thin, you know?" She smiled, trying to get Nomi to smile, too.

But Nomi didn't. "Those boys in the lunchroom? A couple of them, one or two others besides Al, are from Lord's Assembly. And the pastor says violence is wrong. But he also says it's our responsibility to seek out evil and destroy it. He says the right way to do that is through education and through making sure the wrong messages don't get out, like in sex ed and in those books. But I've thought about it a lot, and about Clark's op-ed and your editorial, and I guess maybe I can see now that if the pastor and Clark and I have the right to say we think yours are the wrong messages, it's only fair that you have the right to say you think they're the right ones. And I guess maybe Matt's been trying to show us that we each have a responsibility to do that." She took Jamie's hands. "Are you sure you're all right?"

"Very sure. Especially since you came over. Thank you."

"I was so worried." Nomi squeezed Jamie's hands. "I'll pray

for you, Jamie," she said softly as she hugged her quickly again. "I hope you don't mind."

"I don't mind," Jamie told her, wondering if she did. "It's nice of you. But Nom'," she added as Nomi reached the door, "try to remember that I'm not hurting anyone by being who I am."

Nomi gave Jamie a tentative smile and left.

TWENTY-TWO

Tessa and her family were spending Thanksgiving in Boston, returning Saturday afternoon, when Terry and his parents were due back from visiting Terry's grandparents in Waterville. Ernie, Jamie knew, wouldn't be back till Sunday from the relatives he and his parents were visiting—so at breakfast Saturday morning Jamie said, "I think I'll give Terry a call later, maybe invite him over, okay?"

"Sure," said Mrs. Crawford. "Why don't you ask him to come for dinner? That way we'll get rid of the leftovers faster— Why, Ronnie, what on earth's the matter?"

Jamie and Mr. Crawford both turned to Ronnie, who was staring round-eyed at Jamie. "No!" he said loudly. "No! Don't invite him for dinner. I won't be here; I'll go away . . ."

Jamie looked at him, astonished; he seemed almost hysterical.

"But, Ronnie," said Mrs. Crawford, "you like Terry; you've always liked Terry. Whatever's wrong?"

"I don't like him!" Ronnie shouted. "Not anymore. He— he's . . . I just don't. And you shouldn't either, Jamie."

Jamie saw her parents exchange a glance, saw her father put his hand on her brother's shoulder, heard him say, "Easy, son. Why don't you tell us what's the matter? Terry's an old friend. Why shouldn't Jamie like him anymore?"

No, Jamie thought silently; *no, please, God* . . .

"Because," Ronnie burst out—Jamie saw that he was nearly in tears—"because he—he's a—a faggot, and faggots do things to little kids." He looked reproachfully at Jamie. "To boys especially . . ."

"Ronnie, Ronnie, calm down!" Mr. Crawford got up and put his arms around him. "Calm down. Let's take this one step at a time."

Mrs. Crawford reached over to Jamie and squeezed her hand. "Ronnie," she said gently, "faggot is not a nice word. Do you know what it means?"

"Yes," said Ronnie, sniffling. "I—I think so. It means gay. The kids—all the kids are saying Terry's gay and—and that's why there's trouble about the health education stuff and the newspaper and everything. So you"—he turned to Jamie—"you should stop being friends with him and you should stop the newspaper, maybe, or people will say you're a faggot, too, and . . ."

"Ronnie!" Mr. Crawford said severely. "I think that's enough!"

"No," Jamie said. She'd grown cold suddenly; her whole body had grown cold. But the familiar buzzing in her head had stopped, and she felt pretty sure her hands weren't going to shake as she moved her chair closer to Ronnie's and touched his arm.

"Jamie . . ." began her mother.

"No, Mom," Jamie said. "Let me. Ronnie . . ." She made

her voice as gentle as she could, holding on to it carefully, controlling it, leashing it, she thought; that's it; I'm keeping my voice on a leash, my words, too, maybe. "Ronnie, they're also saying that about me, aren't they? The kids at your school? That I'm gay? Aren't they?"

Ronnie sniffed and nodded. "Y-yeah," he said. "Yeah, they said that. But I said it isn't true. It probably is about Terry, I said, 'cause he's always with that other boy, and they say it about him, too, the other boy. But you've got lots of different friends and everything, so it doesn't matter that you don't really have a boyfriend, or maybe you thought Terry could be your boyfriend, and besides, you're my sister and I'd know. And anyway, you're just not . . ."

Jamie closed her eyes for a moment. Then she looked at her parents over Ronnie's head, trying to ignore the anxiety on their faces, the shock and disbelief on her father's, the loving sympathy on her mother's. "This isn't the way I wanted to do this," she said, still holding her voice on its leash. "But, Ronnie, Mom, Dad—it's true. I'm pretty sure I'm gay. A lesbian. Lesbian's the right word, Ron, for a girl. Not faggot. And Mom's right: faggot's not a nice word. Neither is dyke. I'm sure you've heard that one, too."

Ronnie nodded, tears welling up in his eyes again. "Yes," he said softly. "But you're not . . ."

"It's not the end of the world, Ronnie," Jamie said, aching for him, for herself, too. "It's really not. I'm the same person I always was, really. It's just that you know me better now."

But Ronnie pushed his chair violently away from the table and ran out of the kitchen.

Mr. Crawford got up quickly. "I'll go to him," he said, quickly bending down and kissing Jamie. "I'll talk with him.

It'll be okay, honey; he'll be okay." He took Jamie's face in his hands. "You're still my little girl," he said softly, "and don't you ever, ever forget that. I love you."

Jamie felt tears on her cheeks as she reached up and hugged him. "Thank you," she whispered. "I love you, too."

When Mr. Crawford left, Mrs. Crawford got up and put her arms around Jamie, holding her tightly. "It's okay," she said softly, the way she'd said when Jamie'd been little and had skinned a knee or broken a toy. "It's okay. I'm not surprised, honey, really."

"I've wondered for years," Jamie said. "Terry has, too, about himself, I mean. That's why we became friends at first. Kids teased us and tried to beat us up for the same reason. You know, back in middle school. Elementary, too."

"Those awful fights—and the teasing—it was because of that? You were both so young!"

"Yes. That was the main reason, anyway."

"Oh, Jamie, Jamie," she whispered. "Oh, my sweet child."

"Mom, I'm sorry," Jamie said brokenly, stricken by the sudden pain on her mother's face.

Mrs. Crawford smiled wanly. "No, *I'm* sorry," she said. "I'm sorry that you had to bear all that alone. And"—she looked closely at Jamie—"and if Ronnie's heard—rumors— that must mean some of it's still going on. Some of that cruelty." She paused. "Is it?"

"Some," Jamie admitted, not wanting to burden her mother with details.

"Can you tell me about it?"

"I will if it gets bad enough, Mom," she said carefully. "So far—so far it's okay."

"Jamie, please," her mother said. "Please tell me. Hey," she said, smiling, "kiddo, I can take it! I'd rather know, Jamie," she said more seriously. "I suspect all the fuss about the sex ed curriculum and those burned books hasn't made your life and Terry's any better. And here I thought I was helping prevent just that kind of thing." Her mother rubbed her hands over her face for a moment. "And Tessa's life, too," she said, dropping her hands and looking at Jamie inquiringly, as if a thought had suddenly struck her.

Jamie shook her head. "Tessa and I are just friends," she said evenly. "I think I'm in love with her, but she's straight, so that's kind of that."

"That must be pretty hard on you, honey. Does she know how you feel?"

"She knows I'm gay. I haven't told her I love her. I don't think that would be fair."

"No," said Mrs. Crawford slowly, "I don't suppose it would be. But she's willing to be your friend?"

Jamie nodded.

"She's a pretty special person."

Jamie felt herself smiling. "She is, Mom. She really is."

Much, much later that afternoon, long after Jamie had given her mother a carefully edited account of Brandon and Al's continued harassment, and after Jamie had called Terry but hadn't invited him for dinner, Ronnie knocked on the door to Jamie's room.

"I—um," he began, looking around almost as if he didn't know why he'd come.

He looked so forlorn and so little and so embarrassed that Jamie bent down and hugged him. "Shh," she said. "Shh. It's okay, Ronnie. I know you're sorry. And I know it's not easy having a gay sister. You tell those kids at school whatever you want to, okay? And if they make things too tough, you come and tell me, and I'll go talk to them, or Terry and I will, or Daddy will. Okay?"

Ronnie nodded, clinging to her. "I still love you," he said, his voice muffled. "I don't like that you're gay, but Daddy says it's okay that I don't like it, and that I can love you anyway. And—and I do think you're brave. Mom said kids have teased you about it, and that makes me mad."

"It makes me mad that kids have teased you, too, Ronnie. So we're even."

He smiled up at her. "Mom says the new sex ed thing is supposed to teach people not to tease other people for who they are. And she says you're trying to—to support that in your paper, and she's proud of you. I guess that must be pretty hard, huh? I mean especially if you're gay and all."

"Yeah, it's pretty hard. I'm just trying to do what's right, Ronnie. But it helps to know I've got my family behind me. That means you, too, Ron. You're twenty-five percent of that. A pretty important twenty-five percent, too, the way I look at it."

"Yeah," he said. "Yeah, I know." He wriggled away from her and then paused at the door. "Thirty-three and a third percent, actually," he said, "if you're counting just your supporters and not yourself, too."

December

TWENTY-THREE

The Wilson News-Courier

BUEL CALLS FOR CLEAN SLATE
Health Ed Curriculum under Fire

At last night's Wilson School Committee meeting, member Lisa Buel spoke at length about the recent disruptions at the high school and called for a "clean slate," involving cancellation of condom distribution, along with a new health education curriculum teaching abstinence and omitting any mention of "so-called alternate lifestyles." She also called for "careful monitoring of library purchases," removing "inappropriate" books from the school library, and shelving "controversial materials away from children" in restricted areas in the town library. "The school newspaper," she added, "also needs to be firmly controlled."

Both Elena Snow of the town library and Elizabeth Coats of the three school libraries defended the books removed last fall by Buel's organization, Families for Traditional Values (FTV). According to Snow, those books are now overdue.

In a telephone interview, Coats said, "I stand behind every title we shelve, although I'm always willing to discuss books with parents and other interested citizens."

When asked about the high school newspaper, Principal Ralph Bartholomew replied, "I have been meeting with the paper's staff and with its temporarily suspended adviser, Matt Caggin, about the paper's policies. It is my hope that the school committee will reappoint Mr. Caggin."

After some debate it was decided to hold a public hearing on these matters on Friday, December 11, in the high school auditorium.

Mr. Crawford threw the town paper down in disgust. "That Buel woman is a pain in the neck." He pushed his chair back from the kitchen table and reached for his coffee mug, from which he took a last swallow. "I'd like to keel-haul everyone who voted for her."

"I don't think too many people who voted for her knew what they were getting," Mrs. Crawford said.

Jamie had read the article over her father's shoulder. "I wonder if they'd vote for her now. Are you guys going to that public hearing?"

"You bet we are," her mother said, beginning to clear the breakfast table.

"Me, too." Jamie took her plate to the sink and rinsed it.

Her father frowned, then gave her a quick kiss. "You'd better keep a low profile, though, honey."

"But not so low," Jamie said, picking up her book bag, "that I have to crawl. Right?"

"Right," Mrs. Crawford said emphatically. "I'm so mad I've just about stopped worrying about trying to be fair to people I disagree with!"

Jamie spent most of the weekend—Terry was off someplace with Ernie both Saturday and Sunday when she tried to call him—doing homework and trying to imagine what the public hearing would be like, who would speak at it, what they'd say. And at around 6:00 Monday morning, when the pre-dawn chill made her shiver and pull her quilt up around her neck, it hit her: I could speak—couldn't I? Or couldn't we? The newspaper's been involved in all the issues they're going to be talking about at the meeting; the town should hear from us before they vote.

Jamie's mouth went dry and she shivered again. Standing up and addressing a townwide public hearing would be a lot different from debating at Lord's Assembly or making an announcement in the cafeteria. She wished she hadn't thought of it. But the idea, once it hit her, wouldn't go away, and by the time she got to school, she'd already jotted down some ideas about what to say.

As she turned to go up the school steps, she saw Terry and Ernie walking confidently across the parking lot in animated conversation, hands occasionally brushing together.

Terry looked happy as he and Ernie strode over to her. "Yes," he said, one arm draped proprietarily over Ernie's shoulder, "this is really Ernie, and yes, we spent most of Saturday and all day yesterday together . . ."

"Well into the evening," Ernie added, smiling at Terry.

"Well into the evening."

"Congratulations," said Jamie, trying to change gears, but both boys looked so happy she soon found herself grinning back at them. "So when's the wedding?"

Terry cocked his head as if considering it. "June, I think. Right, Ernie? I always do like a June wedding. The roses are so nice then."

"And there's not much fog." Jamie smiled, hugging him, then gave Ernie a quick kiss on the cheek. "You want me to be a bridesmaid?"

"Mercy, no!" Terry rolled his eyes. "An usher, please." He gestured toward the notes Jamie was still clutching in her hand. "What have we here?"

Jamie explained.

"Cool," Terry said. "But I bet they won't let you, Jamie; it's for voters, that meeting."

"It's a public hearing," she retorted. "And they let us speak at that school committee meeting about Matt. *Us*, Terry; there's no reason why we can't all say something."

But by the end of that day, the others had said they'd rather have Jamie speak for all of them.

The auditorium was mobbed Friday night when Jamie, carrying her notes on a few index cards in her pocket, arrived with her parents and took her seat along with Terry and Ernie, Nomi and Clark, Tessa, and Cindy and Jack in the front of the room, where two rows were reserved for nonvoters. A number of other students were there as well. Brandon, Al, and Sam, who'd returned the Monday after Thanksgiving from being suspended, were among them, plus Karen Hodges. Vicky, who was sitting a little apart from Brandon and his friends, smiled at the newspaper staff; Jamie smiled back.

Soon after Jamie sat down, Morris Just, who had been standing on the stage talking with other members of the school committee, tapped on the mike that had been set up on the lectern and said, "Ladies and gentlemen—folks—I think we should get started. If you want to speak, please go to one of the mikes in the aisles, and remember to let us know who you are. Now, I believe Margaret Crawford has a presentation, and then Lisa Buel. Margaret?"

Jamie listened proudly as her mother traced the history of the health ed curriculum committee, and tried to control her rising anger as Mrs. Buel listed her objections to the curriculum itself. Then, as soon as Mr. Just called for comments from the audience, Matt Caggin stepped up to a mike and introduced himself.

"It's ironic to me," he said, "that we're holding a meeting one of our freedoms allows, in order to decide whether to suspend another freedom. And it shocks me no end that people who purport to support traditional values have so little faith in their own children that they want to withhold knowledge from them."

Mrs. Buel darted to a microphone in the opposite aisle. "Mr. Caggin, I don't believe you have any children. Is that right?"

"That's right, Mrs. Buel. It's also irrelevant. I've taught and advised several hundred kids over the years."

Mr. Just moved swiftly to the lectern. "Let's keep this discussion on the issues, not personalities," he said. "Has anyone anything to say about the health education text and curriculum, or about the condom distribution? Yes? The chair recognizes Anna Pembar."

Nomi's mother had already moved to a mike. "Thank you, Mr. Just. When I ran for the vacant school committee seat against Lisa Buel, I was uneasy about the school's teaching anything except abstinence. But I've been impressed with the realistic point of view expressed in the school paper and in the *Renegade* paper as well. I'm reminded of the ostrich who buries her head in the sand while the forest burns around her. I don't want my children in the fire. I don't think my children will go against my husband's and my teachings, but I have to face the fact that they're new to the intensity of sexual feelings, and I've come to think that maybe they should be taught about safer sex, and that they should have access to condoms, even though I hope they won't have to use them."

Mrs. Pembar stopped and glanced down at some notes she held in her hand, then resumed speaking. "As to alternative lifestyles, I go back to the ostrich again. They exist all around us, and I guess since our kids are exposed to them whether we like it or not, it's a good idea for our kids to be taught to understand them.

"And"—Mrs. Pembar looked around the room, smiling— "in case any of you think what I've just said sounds like a campaign speech, I'll admit that it is. I'll be running for school committee against Lisa Buel again in March, because I believe we need moderates, not extremists, running our schools. Thank you."

About half the audience broke into applause as Mrs. Pembar sat down. Jamie leaned across Tessa and gave Nomi a thumbs-up sign; Nomi mouthed "Thanks" in reply.

Then a man in the back of the room shouted, "Jerome Callet here. I've got something to say."

"Mr. Callet?" said Mr. Just. "Please use a mike, sir. We'll wait."

But Mr. Callet ignored him and went on shouting. "I'm a taxpayer in this town. And I don't want my money going to support what amounts to promoting all kinds of free sex to kids, or to a bunch of liberals or queers who want to force their agendas on other people's children. I don't want the school newspaper to be an opportunity for kids to practice yellow journalism either, or to sound off on stuff they don't know anything about. Think about that before you vote."

Jamie felt her whole body tense as again around half the audience applauded. She glanced at Matt, but his face was turned away toward his wife.

"Anyone else?" Mr. Just asked, his face impassive. "Yes? There in the back. Mr. Davenport?"

"Oh, wow," Tessa whispered to Jamie. "Old Philbert himself! Two white blobs and a wheelchair, remember?"

Jamie nodded and strained to see. But there were too many other people in the way. She heard shuffling, though, and static over the PA system, as if someone was taking a mike from its stand. She imagined the person holding it down low so Mr. Davenport could talk into it.

"Yes," finally came a rasping, breathy voice. "Philbert Davenport here. I just wanted to say that when I went to school in this town long ago we had eight grades in one room, and very few books. I was lucky; my grandfather sent me books—history books, novels, stories, science books—and those books helped me get into college. Helped me hold my own once I got there, too. I wasn't hurt by anything I read, even though some of it was what I guess Mrs. Buel might call immoral. I was helped by it, made wiser. And I think we need to make sure the kids of this town have all kinds of books. I'm going to write out a check this very night to replace the ones those foolish people took away. I understand they haven't yet been returned. Thank you. That's all I have to say."

The static returned momentarily to the PA system, and over it Jamie heard a squeaking sound—the wheelchair, she thought. And over that came applause, not thunderous, but substantial.

"Thank you, Mr. Davenport," Mr. Just said. "And I'm sure the libraries thank you for your generosity. Now," he went on, "I'll take just a few more comments, and then I think we should move to a vote."

Jamie felt her mouth go dry and she started to raise her hand. But she put it down as Mr. Just, looking to one side, said, "Yes, Reverend Donnelly, over there on the right. I see you've found a mike. Go ahead, sir."

"Thank you, Mr. Just," said the pastor of Lord's Assembly. "This controversy has become very disturbing to me. So much personal animosity, so much anger! We need to return to what we all cherish, the values on which this country was founded—God, home, the family—these are things we all hold dear, despite our differences. We are all sinners, after all, in one way or another, and we need to remember that as we try to cast sinful teachings out of our schools. It is sin the Bible teaches us to hate, not each other. Thank you."

Someone called out "Amen!" and there was a burst of enthusiastic applause.

There were a few more speeches on both sides, and finally no hands went up when Mr. Just called for more.

"Go, girl," Terry whispered, poking Jamie.

Jamie, feeling almost as if something outside herself had

pulled her up, had already stood. "Can a nonvoter speak, Mr. Just?" she asked a little shakily, but clearly.

"I don't see why not," Mr. Just replied. "And it would be good to hear from a student or two. Any objections?"

There was a murmur, but no one raised a hand.

"Go ahead," said Mr. Just. "Please identify yourself first. Use the mike up here."

Jamie stepped to the mike and pulled out her notes. She looked at the audience and then, because it was less intimidating, at the exit sign at the rear of the auditorium.

"I'm Jamie Crawford," she began, "and I'm the editor of the Wilson High *Telegraph* and of *The Renegade Telegraph*. Um—anyone who's read the papers knows how I feel about most of the issues, especially the condom one and the First Amendment. You probably also know that I believe a responsible newspaper tries to represent all sides of the issues it covers and a responsible library tries to include information on all issues. Of course, that's not always possible, but it is always possible to try. A responsible school, too, I think, tries to give students information on a wide range of topics so they can make up their own minds and so they can learn to think for themselves. That includes"—she felt her shoulders tense and consciously tried to relax them—"factual information about homosexuality. There are gay kids in our school, as there are in every school. The important thing here is that when you start restricting people's knowledge, letting only some ideas through, you're well on your way to controlling people's minds. Do you really want Wilson to do that? Thank you."

There was a ripple of applause, but before it had a chance to grow, Brandon called out from the second row, "No one wants to read about homosexuality except a bunch of queer kids. Like you," he added in a voice that didn't carry beyond the first two rows. "Homosexuality is evil and sick," he went on, shouting again. "Disgusting!"

Mr. Just banged his gavel on the lectern, but Al's voice rose above it. "God says homosexuality is wrong. Read the Bible!"

"Raise your . . ." Mr. Just shouted angrily, but Tessa interrupted.

"Your god may say it's wrong," she yelled at Al. "But mine doesn't. What about freedom of religion? That's in the First Amendment, too!"

". . . hand," finished Mr. Just. "Any more outbursts like that, all of you," he said severely to Brandon, Al, and Tessa, "and you will be asked to leave. If you have something to contribute"—he looked at Brandon—"please step up to the mike."

Jamie saw Al punch Brandon, but Brandon shook his head.

"Very well. Anyone else? Any other student?"

Again, no one in the front raised a hand, though Jamie saw Karen Hodges whisper to Sam and saw Vicky start to put up her hand and then bring it down again; Vicky shook her head just as Jamie was going to point her out to Mr. Just.

Then, to Jamie's surprise, Nomi's hand went up, and Mr. Just nodded.

"Hello, everyone," Nomi said hesitantly into the mike. "I'm Nomi Pembar." She smiled apologetically and cleared her throat. "I'm a little nervous. My mom's a lot better at making speeches than I am."

"Most folks are nervous about speaking in public," Mr. Just said. "Take your time."

Nomi cleared her throat again. "I just want to say that like my mom I didn't agree with the—the condom distribution at first. I'm still not sure about it. Oh—I'm a senior at Wilson High, I guess I should say, and I'm art editor of the school paper. Mostly I just want to make sure everyone knows that this whole—argument—has led to some pretty ugly things at Wilson High, as well as in the town, as the pastor said. I think calling people names and threatening people is pretty ugly. One of the things the health textbook that's been taken away from us says is that people should respect each other even if they're different. Respecting people doesn't include calling gay kids—or any kids—names, and threatening them or trying to beat them up. That's happened recently at our school. I don't care what a person is, that shouldn't happen anywhere. If the health curriculum can help people understand each other, and the newspaper can help us have a—a dialogue of ideas, sort of, in our school, and the library books can help us learn about and deal with our differences, then I think they all should stay."

Nomi paused for a moment, suddenly looking confused and surprised at finding herself where she was. "Well," she said, "that's it. But I hope you vote for the paper and for the health ed curriculum and for putting those books back in the libraries."

Blushing, Nomi turned away from the lectern; Clark and Jamie both stepped forward and caught her in a bear hug. There was a moment of silence from the audience, and then applause filled the auditorium.

Mr. Just returned to the front of the room. "Thank you, students," he said. "Anyone else from the high school, on the other side of the issue, perhaps?" He looked again at Brandon and Al, both of whom squirmed uncomfortably. Jamie saw Vicky shake her head again.

"Very well," said Mr. Just. "I think we're ready for a vote."

Several voters' hands went up, Mrs. Buel's among them, but Morris Just, with a dismissive gesture, said, "No more, folks. No more. There's a point beyond which additional discussion is useless, and I think we've reached that point. Let's vote now. Just registered voters, please. And remember, these are nonbinding votes. The school committee will ponder the results, plus the comments you've all made tonight, and come to a decision as soon as we can. Now, will all those in favor of retaining the new health education curriculum signify by raising one hand?"

As the votes proceeded one after the other, Jamie tried to count them. But it was impossible to see everyone, even from the front.

"It looks close," Tessa whispered when the voting was finished.

And it was:

Retaining the health ed curriculum:	Yea:	158
	Nay:	159
Restricting access to controversial library books:	Yea:	125
	Nay:	177
	Abstain:	15
Discontinuing the school paper:	Yea:	159
	Nay:	158
Canceling condom distribution:	Yea:	203
	Nay:	114

TWENTY-FOUR

"There's nothing more we can do," Tessa said softly to Jamie late Sunday afternoon; they were walking along Sloan's Beach, watching the waves foam against the rocks. "Everything's out of our hands. And, Jamie, remember, the school committee can't shut down the *Renegade*, even if they can shut down the *Telegraph*. So either way, we still win, sort of."

"Only sort of. Who wants to live in this town if Lisa Buel's ideas win?"

"I do." Tessa swung her arms wide. "I wanted to go back to Boston when I first moved here, but now I love the sea and the fresh air and the lobster boats and the marsh grass, and I love the friends I've found here—especially one. I'm proud to be your friend, Jamie Crawford, and I hope I'll always be your friend." She grinned. "Someday you'll start a newspaper that'll be known all over the country. And maybe you'll let me be a staff photographer, and then we'll write a book together—oh, wow, Jamie! Don't we have an essay to do? We've forgotten all about that. It must be time for another!"

"You're right," Jamie said. "It is. An early-winter essay."

"Late fall–early winter," Tessa corrected. "It's not officially winter yet." She glanced around. "Right. Here's a good place to start. Come on. There's still just enough light. Let's go get my camera. Race you to the car."

"It's gonna be a tense day, folks," Terry said nervously Monday morning when he and Ernie met Jamie and Tessa outside school. "Announcement-of-our-fate day, assuming the school committee's made up their minds. And a brand-new week facing our growing public as Wilson High's two-and-only almost-as-good-as-out faggots. But we can take whatever comes, right, Ern?" He gave Ernie a mock-jock poke in the ribs.

Ernie dropped his voice an octave. "Yeah, man. You know it's weird," he went on in his normal voice, "but I'm not as scared as I used to be. It's sort of a relief, you know? Not to have to pretend so much."

"Yes," Jamie said. "Poor Nomi, though. She said she realized afterward that what she said pretty much cleared up any doubts Brandon and Al or any other kids might have had about us . . ."

"Oh, come on!" Tessa exclaimed. "Excuse me, but what doubts, you know? Besides, you started the process yourself, in your speech."

"That's what I told her," Jamie went on, "and Nomi said she knew that, but she still hoped we weren't mad."

"Mad?" said Terry, making his eyes round. "*Moi?*" He turned to Ernie. "*Toi? Et toi?*" he added, looking at Jamie.

Jamie laughed. "*Non, monsieur, je ne suis pas* . . . what's mad? Anyway, I told her we weren't, and she hugged me and I think it's all okay. Still, I'm not sure I'm dying to run into Brandon and Al today. Or Karen or Sam, for that matter."

"True." As the first bell rang, Terry put his hand on the small of Ernie's back and pushed him gently forward. "However. Squaring their shoulders," he announced grandly, "the two brave faggots marched undaunted into the fray. Onward, comrade!"

"You okay?" Tessa asked when Terry and Ernie had left.

"Yeah, I think so." Jamie looked after them. "And I sure hope Ernie really is, too."

The second bell rang, and Tessa grimaced. "Here we go!" She gave Jamie's shoulder a quick pat. "If the two brave faggots can march undaunted into the fray, I guess the brave— um, lesbian—and her straight best friend can, too. Ready?"

"Ready. But do you think I could skip opening my locker? I know it's been okay since Brandon and company came back, but after that meeting . . ."

"No, you can't skip it. Might as well get it over with."

But Jamie's locker was fine, as was Tessa's, which Jamie suddenly worried about, and the worst that Brandon and his friends did, besides stare and make inaudible comments, was to surreptitiously give Jamie and Tessa the finger whenever they passed them in the halls. Tessa sailed regally by as if she didn't notice, and Jamie told herself she was doing the same.

The atmosphere all morning was strained, as if everyone in the building was on hold, waiting for the school committee's decision. Terry cracked his knuckles in every class Jamie had with him, and Ernie seemed tense again when Terry brought him to the newspaper table at lunch.

"How's it been?" Jamie asked, moving her chair to accommodate him and smiling at Nomi, who waved at her from where she was sitting with Clark. "Still okay?" Nomi mouthed, and Jamie mouthed back, "Yes, fine."

"It's been no worse than last week," Terry answered. "Mostly stares."

"Someone said, 'When's the wedding?'" Ernie told them, "and a couple of kids flapped their wrists at us."

"Pretty standard stuff." Terry made his voice lower as Ernie had earlier. "Like I said, we can take it."

"You are all so brave," Cindy said—and then the PA system crackled. Jamie crossed her fingers as the room fell unnaturally silent, except for Jack's whispered "Here we go, folks. I hope."

Terry sat down again, and Nomi, with Clark at their table nearby, shot Jamie an anxious look.

The PA system crackled once more, and Mr. Bartholomew's voice echoed through the room: "Students and faculty, your attention, please. I've now heard from Mr. Just, who, as you know, is chairman of the school committee. The committee's decision is as follows:

"The health education course is canceled for the remainder of this year, as is condom distribution. A new special committee will be appointed to rewrite the curriculum at all levels and choose new textbooks, both to be in place for next year if the new school committee approves of them after the March election, and another new committee, including the school nurse, will gather data on the experiences other schools have had with condom distribution.

"The school libraries will not shelve any books that deal in any way, pro or con, with homosexuality. Any books on that subject found in the school libraries will be donated to the public library, where, the head librarian tells me, they will be available, although possibly on restricted shelves. That decision, which is up to the public library staff and trustees, has not yet been made.

"The school newspaper is canceled for the rest of this school year, but will be reinstituted, with an adviser to be appointed by the new school committee, next fall.

"I know that some of these decisions will be hard for many of you to swallow. But for the moment, they must stand. The school committee asked me to say that they based their decisions on the votes recorded at the meeting last week, and it's obvious that's true, although two of those votes were almost ties. Now, please go to your classes, in which, I'm sure, many of you will want to discuss what you've heard."

Jamie was hardly aware that Tessa's hand was resting on hers or that Ernie was shaking his head. Cindy was tearing her napkin into shreds, and Terry was pounding his fist into his hand; Jack's mouth was wide-open in obvious disbelief, and Nomi, looking stricken, had stood up and was moving toward them. The words *No paper—no paper—no paper* thundered in Jamie's mind.

TWENTY-FIVE

"So," said Matt after school, when Jamie, Terry, Tessa, Nomi, Jack, and Cindy found him cleaning out his desk in the newspaper office. "What's your strategy?"

Jamie glanced at the others, none of whom seemed to have anything to say. "I don't know yet." She tried to pull herself together. "But I guess we'll go on with the *Renegade*. Expand it, maybe."

"And I guess," said Terry, "since we're not afraid of opinion, that we need to do whatever we can to get Mrs. Buel out and Nomi's mother in."

"There's one other person whose term is up," Matt said. His voice was muffled; he was bent over, rummaging in a bottom drawer. "Helen Rush. She's an FTV member and she's running again."

"Anyone know who's running against her?" Jack asked.

"My dad," Tessa told them, grinning. "He was really mad about that meeting, and he's on our side."

Cindy grinned back. "So the *Renegade* needs to—what's it called? Support?"

"Endorse," Matt said, straightening up.

"Yeah, that's it. We need to endorse Mrs. Pembar and Mr. Gillespie." She looked hopefully at Matt. "I don't suppose you can help any, right?"

"Right. I wish I could. I'll reapply for the *Telegraph* job after the March election. But meanwhile, I can't violate the school committee's decision. Besides, gang, you really don't need me. You may need more staff, though, I think, if you're going to do a really thorough job . . ."

"I'll help," Nomi said, "now that the *Telegraph*'s gone and if the *Renegade* expands." She smiled at Jamie. "As long as we can publish more than one side of things as the *Telegraph* did, and as long as we can agree to disagree."

"You bet!" Jamie said, giving her a quick hug across the shoulders. "Especially in an expanded paper."

"I've got a friend," Jack said, "who does great cartoons, plus he's not bad as a writer either."

"And there's a girl in my English class," Cindy put in, "who does really good objective essays."

"Great," Jamie said. "Are you sure they'll all be willing?"

Cindy and Jack exchanged a glance. "Sure," Jack said.

"After all," Cindy added, "we juniors need more training if we're going to run next year's official paper."

Matt saluted them as he went out the door, carrying a canvas bag of his belongings. "Good luck," he said. "I know you're all going to be just fine."

March

TWENTY-SIX

THE RENEGADE TELEGRAPH

Published occasionally, independently of the Wilson High *Telegraph*,
and expanded in that paper's temporary absence

Buel Out; Books In!

March 18—Anna Pembar roundly defeated Lisa Buel in yesterday's townwide school committee election, by a vote of 583 to 118. Helen Rush, the other member whose term was up, was also defeated, 580 to 121, by Theodore Gillespie.

In a written statement made public after the election, Buel said, "I'm thankful to the town for my opportunity to serve on the school committee these past few months, and I hope to continue working for the benefit of Wilson's young people through Families for Traditional Values. It is only through strong families, strong churches, and an adherence to the principles taught in the Bible and handed down through the ages that this nation will be able to save itself from decadence and moral disaster. FTV will continue to labor cheerfully toward that end."

Mrs. Buel's successor, Anna Pembar, said in a phone interview, "Lisa Buel and the folks in FTV are good, sincere people, and I hope we will be able to work with them in the coming year. Even though our views differ as to methods, many of our goals are similar."

In his campaign, Theodore Gillespie, the newly elected school committee member replacing Helen Rush, said, "The school committee, like the school itself, needs to concern itself with education, not morality. Morality needs to be taught in the home. In school, especially high school, kids need access to as many ideas and cultures as possible. It's my intention to do everything I can to ensure that Wilson's students have access to the free marketplace of ideas."

Morris Just, who will continue as school committee chairman until the end of the school year, when the committee will hold their annual election of officers, told the *Renegade* that the committee's first order of business will be to review the matters voted on in the public hearing last December. They will be reviewing the subcommittee's recommendations, made in late February, for changes in the health education textbooks and curricula, studying the data gathered about the effects of condom availability at other schools, receiving applications for faculty adviser to the Wilson High *Telegraph*, discussing policy matters with the school librarian, and making decisions based on their findings.

"The opinion of the majority is important," Mr. Just

said. "But the majority must never be allowed to tyrannize the minority—nor must the minority be allowed to tyrannize the majority. We on the school committee want to ensure that all voices are heard and considered, and that Wilson's young people are given the best, most professional education we can provide. I think we'll be able to find a way to accommodate the wishes of all parents when it comes to controversial programs and materials."

Mrs. Elena Snow, head librarian of the Wilson Public Library, and Mrs. Elizabeth Coats, of the Wilson school libraries, have told the *Renegade* that the books on sex education and homosexuality that were checked out of the libraries last winter and never returned have been replaced through a generous donation from Philbert Davenport. Those belonging to the public library will be reshelved. The newly elected school committee will appoint a book review committee to consider reshelving those belonging to the school libraries.

"Okay?" Jamie passed around several copies of the article. "Comments? Changes?"

"Perfect," said Cindy. Jack, sitting next to her, nodded.

"I'm not sure the library paragraph really works, though," Jamie said. "Seems a little tacked on."

"Oh, it's okay." Terry handed his copy to Ernie, who had come to the *Renegade*'s meeting, as had Clark. "Don't fuss, Jamie. Besides, it's not long enough to be a separate story."

"Yeah, but how about expanding it to a sidebar?"

Tessa reread the article. "It could be one, but I don't think it's necessary. After all, it really is part of the same story."

"Maybe it needs a stronger transition," Jamie said, frowning. "You know, leading into it."

Nomi put her arm around her. Winking at Clark, she said, "Leave it, Jamie. I agree it's perfect the way it is." She looked at her watch. "Are we all going to Georgeport or not? Because we've only got an hour and a half till the movie starts, and since there are eight of us going on this celebration and we want to sit together . . ."

Jamie wriggled partway around under Nomi's arm. "You *agree*, Nom'?" she asked with mock surprise.

But Nomi just smiled. "Yes, Jamie. I agree."

The next afternoon Jamie sat on her favorite rock on Sloan's Beach, the yellow notebook from her private box on her knee. But it wasn't a private box anymore; she'd decided to keep it on her desk now, out in the open.

I wish I could think it's over, the whole fuss about sex education and the newspaper. But I guess it isn't. Even though Mrs. Buel and that other FTV person are no longer on the school committee, and even though the library books have been replaced, FTV's still going to push for their ideas, and people like Brandon are still going to be rotten to people like Ernie and Terry and me, and people like Ernie's parents are still going to be so homophobic they make it impossible for their own kids to be honest with them about who they really are. At least Ernie's able to be himself at the Gages', but I know it hurts him terribly not to be able to tell his own family who he really is. I think Terry and I are very lucky, and I know both of us worry sometimes about Ernie, even though I think he'll probably be okay. He really has gotten a lot stronger this year—but I hope someday he'll finally be able to come out to his parents.

*Have I? Gotten stronger, I mean? I guess so. I know more about
who I am, I think. Now I've got to stop falling in love with people
who can't love me back—well, who can't love me back in the same
way. I'm glad Tessa still wants to be my friend. I think I'll always
be a little sad that she can't be more than that, but knowing Terry
and Ernie has made me believe I really will find someone someday.
Yeah. I'm pretty sure I will.*

*I used to think that all you had to do to right a wrong was write
about it clearly, telling people what the problem was and what the
facts were, and then people would see the truth of what you were
saying and would fix the problem. I know the <u>Renegade</u> had a lot of
influence on what happened this year—at least I think it did—but I
also know it didn't solve the problem. Maybe nothing can. Maybe
truth is a lot more elusive than I thought. FTV believes it's
arguing for the truth, and I believe I am, and we each believe our
facts are right. I'm not sure how to reconcile that. Maybe it can't be
reconciled. Of course that's why it's vital for newspapers to give both
sides.*

*But isn't it also important for a newspaper—or a person—to
take a firm, honest stand about their beliefs?*

*I'm pretty sure of one thing: that people, no matter what they
believe or what their differences are, have to be able to live together
without hurting each other. Maybe that's the one true truth, the
one I most want to work toward for the rest of my life . . .*

Jamie snapped her head around, startled. Tessa had come
up quietly behind her, smiling, and was standing there in her
red cape, her camera bag slung over her shoulder.

"Come on, friend," she said. "We've got a spring photo essay to start putting together."